"Chance!" *Joy ga...*
doing here!"

"It looks like I'll be sleeping here tonight."

"There isn't room in the bunkhouse?" she asked.

"Yes, but how could I tell the men I couldn't sleep with my wife? Don't worry, I'll sleep on the floor."

"You can't. You have to be on a horse tomorrow. You take the bed."

"You need your rest, too, Joy," he said. "I've slept on the ground before."

Stubborn man. "Chance, it's a large bed. I don't see anything wrong with you sleeping on top of the covers—on your side."

"Lady, you're playing with fire."

"Not if we don't let anything happen. All I'm offering is one side of the bed."

He watched her for what seemed like an eternity, then said, "I'll take it."

Dear Reader,

Get Caught Reading. It sounds slightly scandalous, romantic and definitely exciting! I love to get lost in a book, and this month we're joining the campaign to encourage reading everywhere. Share your favorite books with your partner, your child, your friends. And be sure to get caught reading yourself!

The popular ROYALLY WED series continues with Valerie Parv's *Code Name: Prince*. King Michael is still missing—but there's a plan to rescue him! In *Quinn's Complete Seduction* Sandra Steffen returns to BACHELOR GULCH, where Crystal finally finds what she's been searching for—and more....

Chance's Joy launches Patricia Thayer's exciting new miniseries, THE TEXAS BROTHERHOOD. In the first story, Chance Randell wants to buy his lovely neighbor's land, but hadn't bargained for a wife and baby! In *McKinley's Miracle*, talented Mary Kate Holder debuts with the story of a rugged Australian rancher who meets his match.

Susan Meier is sure to please with *Marrying Money*, in which a small-town beautician makes a rich man rethink his reasons for refusing love. And Myrna Mackenzie gives us *The Billionaire Is Back*, in which a wealthy playboy fights a strong attraction to his pregnant, single cook!

Come back next month for the triumphant conclusion to ROYALLY WED and more wonderful stories by Patricia Thayer and Myrna Mackenzie. Silhouette Romance always gives you stories that will touch your emotions and carry you away....

Be sure to *Get Caught Reading!*

Mary-Theresa Hussey

Mary-Theresa Hussey
Senior Editor

Please address questions and book requests to:
Silhouette Reader Service
U.S.: 3010 Walden Ave., P.O. Box 1325, Buffalo, NY 14269
Canadian: P.O. Box 609, Fort Erie, Ont. L2A 5X3

Chance's Joy

PATRICIA THAYER

SILHOUETTE *Romance*

Published by Silhouette Books

America's Publisher of Contemporary Romance

To My Nieces and Nephews
Nora, Danielle, Sarah, Lydgia, Judy, Hannah, Malachi, Stephen, Arron,
Hannah and little Josh. Nikki, Travis and Anthony.
You too, Glenn.

You're a great bunch, and I had a wonderful time getting to know you
all. Thanks for hanging out with your Aunt Pat.
See you at the next Greiner wedding.

 SILHOUETTE BOOKS

ISBN 0-373-19518-4

CHANCE'S JOY

Copyright © 2001 by Patricia Wright

This edition published by arrangement with Harlequin Books S.A.

Visit Silhouette at www.eHarlequin.com

Printed in U.S.A.

Books by Patricia Thayer

Silhouette Romance

Just Maggie #895
Race to the Altar #1009
The Cowboy's Courtship #1064
Wildcat Wedding #1086
Reilly's Bride #1146
The Cowboy's Convenient Bride #1261
*Her Surprise Family #1394
*The Man, the Ring, the Wedding #1412
†Chance's Joy #1518

Silhouette Special Edition

Nothing Short of a Miracle #1116
Baby, Our Baby! #1225
*The Secret Millionaire #1252
Whose Baby Is This? #1335

*With These Rings
†The Texas Brotherhood

PATRICIA THAYER

has been writing for fourteen years and has published over ten books with Silhouette. Her books have been nominated for the National Readers' Choice Award, Virginia Romance Writers of America's Holt Medallion and a prestigious RITA Award. In 1997 *Nothing Short of a Miracle* won the *Romantic Times Magazine* Reviewers' Choice Award for Best Special Edition.

Thanks to the understanding men in her life—her husband of twenty-eight years, Steve, and her three sons—Pat has been able to fulfill her dream of writing romance. Another dream is to own a cabin in Colorado, where she can spend her days writing and her evenings with her favorite hero, Steve. She loves to hear from readers. You can write to her at P.O. Box 6251, Anaheim, CA 92816-0251.

All underlined places are fictitious.

Chapter One

Chance Randell had waited a long time for his dream. He just had to be patient a while longer. But patience had never been easy for him, he thought, as he rode his buckskin horse, Ace, along the fence that bordered the Circle B Ranch to the deserted Kirby place.

He looked out over the rolling hills of West Texas. Last week's rain had only added to the rich, emerald hue of the lush spring grass. Ancient oak trees spotted the landscape, their large branches capable of shading herds of mama cows even on the hottest June and July days.

Chance pushed the Stetson back from his forehead as he shifted in the saddle. "Sure is some prime grazing land," he said into the warm April breeze. "And soon, it's gonna be mine."

Just months ago, Chance had learned from Lillian Kirby's lawyer that her only nephew had died, but the search was on for other relatives to stake claim to the place.

If there were any, Chance bet they'd be city folk who didn't want any part of running a cattle ranch. And he was going to make damn sure when—or if—anyone showed up, he'd be first in line to make an offer on the ranch. One way or the other, he was going to get this place. Yeah, that was his plan all right.

For as long as he could remember, Chance had wanted his own ranch. Most of his life he'd lived on the Circle B. Ever since Hank Barrett had seen fit to drag him and his incorrigible brothers from a life in the foster-care system.

A slow smile creased Chance's mouth as he thought about the man who had believed in those wild Randell brothers. Their mother had died several years ago, and they hadn't had any options until Hank had opened his home to all of them. It had been the last chance for the trio everyone else had given up on.

Back then Chance had had more attitude than brains. Some people thought he still did. For the most part, Chance never cared what other people thought. They were going to think the worst just because he had the last name Randell. It didn't matter that he'd been the Circle B's foreman for the past ten years, or that he'd trained some of the finest quarter horses in the area. There were people who'd never forgotten that their father, Jack Randell, had been sent to prison. Chance and his brothers had spent most of their lives trying to pay for their father's sins.

"To hell with them all," he cursed, and Ace danced sideways sensing his rider's mood swing.

Wait until he had his own place. He'd show everyone. Determined to have his dream, Chance had managed to save nearly everything he'd made over the years.

Even though Hank had always wanted the brothers to think of the ranch as their home, Chance wanted something of his own. At nearly thirty-four, he wanted a home. Not that he had anyone to share it with. His thoughts drifted back to a time when he'd thought that love was possible. But Belinda Reed had had other ideas. Her only interest had been to have a good time with one of the wild Randell boys.

Chance tightened his grip on the saddle horn as he thought about the fateful summer he'd been made a fool of. It had taken him years, but he'd learned all kinds of tricks to keep his emotions under control. And his practiced stony gaze could shield his hurt from just about everyone. He wasn't going to let anyone get close enough to hurt him again.

He pushed away the memories and gave Ace a slight nudge. He rode through the gate and stopped at the barn about a hundred yards from the old house. Might as well check on the winter feed. A few years back he'd arranged a deal with Lillian Kirby to use her barn to store feed. It had also been an excuse for Hank or Chance to check up on the old woman who'd lived here alone until her death about twelve months ago.

Chance swung his leg off his horse and tied the reins to the rusted metal fence. He glanced toward the house and saw that the paint was faded and starting to peel. He could easily take care of the problem in a few days. Some scraping and prepping, and the house could be ready to paint. White. He'd always wanted a white ranch house. The big wraparound porch sagged a little, but that could be taken care of, too.

He walked around to the barn door and discovered it open. Great, had kids been in here again? Inside, he examined the bags of feed and found them untouched. That was when he heard the noise.

It was more of a cry. Like an animal in pain. He moved down the aisle between the empty stalls toward the tack room, where the noise got louder. Carefully and slowly, not wanting an injured animal to attack him, he opened the door. What he saw was a shock. A woman. A very pregnant woman doubled over in pain.

Joy Spencer's timing couldn't have been worse. She'd thought she had everything figured out. But her plans hadn't included her baby deciding to come two weeks early. She'd had back pain most of the morning, but thought it had been caused by the long drive here, not labor. She had to get some help. Once the pain subsided she stood up and tried to walk, but before she could make it to the door another pain hit her, making her cry out again.

"Oh, no," she groaned, when she felt a gush of warm water running down her legs. She was in big trouble now. Sinking down onto the wooden bench, she managed to ride out the contraction.

"God, please help me," she whispered as she tried to catch her breath.

"Guess you're stuck with me instead."

She jerked around to find a tall man with shoulders so wide they blocked the doorway. His long legs were encased in jeans and brown leather chaps. A black cowboy hat sat low on his head, nearly covering a pair of piercing gray eyes.

"Who are you?" she gasped.

He came further into the room. "Name's Chance

Randell. A neighbor. By the looks of things, you could use some help." He knelt down beside her.

She nodded. "It's my baby. It's early. Please, can you get me to the hospital?"

"Only if you have a car," he said. "I rode over here on a horse."

"My keys are in my purse—" she groaned as another pain raced through her. Joy gripped the man's shirt and cried out. This was all happening too fast.

"Okay, ma'am, try to take a slow easy breath," he coaxed.

Joy did as he directed, and finally the pain faded. He helped her to the cot in the corner of the room where she collapsed and closed her eyes.

"I'll be right back." The stranger started to get up and she grabbed him again.

"No, don't leave me."

"I'm not going anywhere, ma'am. Just need to get my cellular phone from the saddle bags. I'll call an ambulance."

Joy was too exhausted to do anything but nod and whisper, "Just hurry."

Chance ran outside and tore his saddle bags off Ace. His hands were trembling as he took out his phone and punched in the emergency numbers. When someone answered, he nearly yelled in the dispatcher's ear. "I need an ambulance at the Kirby place out off Highway 56. A woman is about to have a baby."

Several moments later, they had patched him into the hospital. A doctor came on the line. "Hello, I'm Dr. Hager. Are you the husband?"

"No, I'm a neighbor, Chance Randell. I just found the woman..." Damn. Wasn't this his lucky day?

"Well, it looks like you're all she has for the moment. How far apart are her pains?"

"Not far. A few minutes at the most."

"Okay, Chance, I'll stay on the line with you until help arrives."

"Thanks. My only experience with birthing is with the four-legged variety." Chance hurried into the tack room just as another pain gripped the tiny blond woman. He went to her and let her grasp his hand until the pain finally subsided.

She looked at him, fear etched on her face. "They're not going to get here in time, are they?"

Chance forced a smile. "Hey, I've got it under control, blue eyes. I've got Dr. Hager right here on the line." He handed the phone to her. She talked with the doctor and answered his questions.

She gave Chance back the phone. "He wants to talk to you."

"Look, Chance," the doctor began. "I want you to make sure she stays calm. Just in case things speed up and she gives birth before the paramedics get there, you've got to help her breathe through the pains."

And just how was he supposed to do that? Cows didn't need this kind of help. "Sure, Doc," he said, more confidently than he really felt.

The woman grabbed his arm again and groaned as another contraction began.

"Breathe, breathe." He puffed out his cheeks and started panting rapidly. Finally she got the picture and followed his lead as the pain faded out.

Three minutes later another pain struck. They repeated the same breathing technique until she collapsed exhausted on the cot.

Chance took out his bandanna and wiped the moisture from her face. "You're doing just great," he said.

She looked at him skeptically, clearly not convinced. "It wasn't supposed to be like this. The baby's early."

"That happens. Is there anyone else I can call? Your mother, husband…?"

She shook her head. "No, my husband is dead. It's just me…and the baby." He didn't question her when she closed her eyes. But not for long, he thought as another pain began.

"Oohh, I need to push."

"Breathe," he pleaded with her.

Chance hung in there, coaxing her, wondering why the hell a pregnant woman was out here all alone. If he hadn't come by she'd have really been in trouble.

"Thank you," she whispered.

"Ssh. Save your strength," he said and got her some water from a bottle in his bag. While she rested, he raised the phone to his ear. "Look, doc, where the hell is the ambulance?"

"It's en route. Chance, just concentrate on your patient. I have to know if she's crowning."

Chance swallowed. He knew there was only one way to find that out.

He put down the phone and turned around. "Look, ma'am, the doctor says I need to examine you. I'm sorry. I'll try and make it quick."

Her eyes got big and wide, then she nodded. "Go ahead." She looked so tiny, so fragile with her oversized shirt and long skirt, her belly rounded. After pulling off her panties, she bent her knees and draped her skirt over her legs. Another contraction hit her. "I've got to push again," she cried.

"Don't. Not yet. Breathe," Chance ordered, then he gave a quick glance under her skirt and saw the baby's head. He grabbed the phone. "Okay, doc. We have a head showing."

"All right. You'll need a clean knife and something to wrap the baby in."

"Hold on." Chance searched through his bag and found a towel and washcloth. In the small first aid kit there was some disinfectant and small bandages. Then he dug into his jeans pocket to find his knife.

"Yeah, I have a small towel and some disinfectant." He glanced around the room. "But nothing to wrap the baby in."

"Then take off your shirt and use that. Wash your hands in the disinfectant and hurry, because on the next contraction, she's going to have to push again. And you need to help guide the baby's head...."

Chance dropped the phone and did as the doctor directed. He finished just as she cried out again. "All right, blue eyes, let's get this baby born. Push."

The blonde bore down hard with a groan, her face red from the exertion.

"Hey, you're doing just fine," a surprised Chance said as he cradled the baby's tiny head in his hands. "Give one more big push. Come on, your baby needs you," he coaxed.

Tears rolled from her eyes as she panted. "I can't."

"Yes, you can," he argued. "Your baby needs you."

That did it. With the next pain, she gave it all she had. And Chance could only gasp as the tiny infant slid out into his shaking hands. Already the baby girl was crying. "Hey, you got yourself a daughter," he whispered.

All at once the woman began to cry in earnest. Chance was busy cutting and tying the cord with his disinfected pocketknife. Once done, he wrapped the baby in his chambray shirt. "Wish it could be pink, little one." He held her for a moment, watching as the tiny bundle looked up at him, her eyes open and trusting, just like her mother's. Something tightened in his chest.

"Is she all right?"

The woman's voice brought him back to reality. "Oh, yeah, I'd say she's perfect." He carefully handed her to her mother.

"Oh, she's beautiful," she cried.

"She's a keeper all right," Chance agreed as his gaze locked with the mother's bright blue eyes, then turned his attention to the newborn. Unable to resist, he touched his finger to her soft cheek in wonder over this miracle he'd helped bring into world.

Just then the sound of the ambulance pierced the silence. "Looks like help has arrived."

"I think my daughter and I had all the help we needed. Thank you."

Chance realized that the doctor was still on the phone. "Hey, it's a girl," he said. "She looks fine. The ambulance just pulled up."

"Chance, you did a good job. Congratulations."

"Thanks, doc, for all your help."

"You're the one who did all the work. Tell the mother that I'll be waiting for the two of them at the hospital."

Chance hung up and smiled. Then the paramedics rushed in, and he stepped aside.

Realizing mother and child didn't need him anymore, disappointment rushed through him. Well, what did he expect? What decent woman would have anything to do with a Randell? He stiffened and turned and walked out. Besides he didn't need any strays. The last thing he needed was to get involved with a widowed woman and her kid.

Joy was exhausted, but so happy as she looked down at her new baby daughter, Kathryn Rose.

"Oh, Blake, she's beautiful," she whispered. Tears clogged her throat at the thought of her husband. It had been only seven months since his sudden death, and although the shock of his passing had lessened with time, she would always miss him. Blake had been her friend, her family, as she was his. Joy glanced down at Katie Rose again. But she wasn't alone anymore. Never again was she going to be without family. Mother and daughter had each other now and nothing was going to separate them.

The young, dark-haired paramedic approached the ambulance. "We'll be transporting you shortly, ma'am," he said.

"Thank you," Joy answered.

"I'm not the one you should thank," the man said. "I'd say the cowboy had everything under control by the time we got here."

Joy glanced out the open doors of the ambulance, and spotted the big man standing back from the attendants. His hands rested on his lean hips, and she could see the evidence of the ordeal of the birth on his damp T-shirt and jeans. Her gaze rose to the hard planes of his face and his steel-gray eyes, now hidden by a dusty cowboy hat.

She motioned for him to come to the ambulance and watched his slow, deliberate gait as he made his way toward her. Joy smiled to herself, as something told her this cowboy did things his way. A tingle erupted deep in her stomach and a blush spread across her cheeks, as she remembered that just moments ago they'd shared the intimacy of her baby's birth. She recalled his encouraging words as he helped her through her labor, and the tenderness of his touch as he brought her daughter into the world. She didn't want to think about what would have happened if he hadn't shown up.

The cowboy stopped next to the door and removed his hat, revealing the brown-streaked hair Joy had focused on during her pains.

"Looks like you're all fixed up," he said, his expression cool. The change in his mood surprised her.

"I'm fine. And my daughter is perfect. I'm sorry that I had to put you through this."

"No problem, ma'am. Glad I could help."

"I'm very happy you were here, too. I'll always be grateful."

Chance couldn't stop looking at the pretty woman on the gurney. Her long blond hair was still damp, and little ringlets curled around her face. Her large blue eyes were the color of the bluebonnets that grew wild along the Texas hillsides. Realizing where his thoughts were headed, he quickly glanced away. "Like I said, just being neighborly."

"So you're my neighbor?" she asked.

"Out here, we all watch out for one another. It's a good thing you found the Kirby place. It's just too bad it was deserted."

"I was purposely looking for Lillian Kirby's place."

An uneasy feeling suddenly washed over Chance.

He remembered that the lawyer handling Miss Kirby's
will had said that her nephew was deceased, and they
hadn't been able to locate any other relatives. Surely
this couldn't be another...? He shook away the
thought. "I don't see why, no one has lived here for
nearly a year."

The woman smiled and looked at her baby. "That's
going to change soon."

Chance froze. What did she mean by that? All of a
sudden the paramedic started to close the door.
"Wait!" Chance stopped him and glared at the
woman. "What do you mean?"

"That just as soon as Katie Rose and I get released
from the hospital we'll be moving in."

She was going to live here? "Look Mrs.—" He
stopped, realizing he didn't even know her name. "I
guess we never got to introductions. I'm Chance Randell from the Circle B."

She smiled sweetly. "Nice to meet you Mr. Randell.
I'm Lil's great-niece, Joy Kirby Spencer."

Chance couldn't say a word as he let go of the
doors, and the attendant pulled them shut. He stared
after the ambulance as it drove off down the gravel
road, watching until the vehicle finally disappeared,
along with his dreams.

Chapter Two

Hell, the last time Chance had been in a hospital was when his friend, Huey Johns, had been tossed off a bull at the rodeo. He'd *never* visited a maternity ward.

Chance got off the elevator that evening with a bouquet of flowers in one hand and his hat in the other, ready to have a little talk with Mrs. Spencer. But when he started past the nursery, he found himself stopping. Just for a quick glance at the kid, he told himself.

He located the clear, plastic crib with Spencer written at the base and was mesmerized by the sleeping baby wrapped in a soft pink blanket. Her tiny fists were clenched, and her little mouth was in a pout, occasionally making a slow sucking motion. A crown of downy hair covered her head, partially hidden by a pink cap.

Chance heard voices behind him and realized he'd been standing there staring like a silly fool. A sudden sadness overtook him as he thought about his solitary life. Here he was, a bachelor who'd never thought much about having his own family. The ranch had kept him busy enough so he didn't have much time to think about what he didn't have. Ever since his brothers had left, it had only been him, Hank and Ella. Not that he would mind if his brothers decided to come home.

Chance took one last look at the baby. No, he wouldn't mind at all. He continued down the hall to handle the business that had brought him here in the first place. Talking one city lady out of a ranch.

At the nurses' station, he was given the new mother's room number and quickly found the two-bed room. Joy Spencer was in the first cubicle. He hesitated when he noticed she was asleep, and couldn't help studying her. Her long blond hair seemed to have a life of its own, the wayward curls framing her oval face. His gaze lowered to the print hospital gown. The petite woman didn't look like she'd just given birth, he thought, recalling a few hours earlier when he'd shared the experience with her. All at once his throat went bone-dry, and he couldn't seem to swallow.

Damn! What was he doing, staring at a woman, and a new mother at that? He'd better just leave and come back tomorrow. Looking for a place to put the flowers, Chance tried to lay them down on the table next to the bed, but only managed to knock over a drinking glass. The plastic tumbler bounced twice on the tiled floor before he could retrieve it.

When he stood up, he found a pair of deep-blue eyes on him. He felt the heat rush up his neck. "Ah...sorry. I didn't mean to wake you." He pointed toward the hall. "The nurse said I could come in."

Joy Spencer smiled, and his stomach tightened.

"It's okay. I'm glad you came by, Mr. Randell."

"Call me Chance."

Joy couldn't help but stare at her rescuer. This man who had so confidently taken care of her and Katie seemed all thumbs now. "Chance…I want to thank you again for everything you did today."

The tall rugged cowboy shook his head of neatly combed sandy hair. "No need, ma'am. Just glad it all worked out." He gave her a half smile that showed off even white teeth. "I've never delivered a baby before. I mean, I've helped a few calves and colts into the world, but never a…baby."

"Well, this is a first for me, too," she said. "Did you see Katie in the nursery?"

He nodded. "I got a quick look. I picked her out right away."

A short silence stretched between them, then Joy glanced at the lovely spring flowers he gripped in his hand. "Are those for me?"

"Oh, yeah. I was just going to leave 'em. But I couldn't find anything to put them in."

"You can use the water pitcher."

This time Chance managed to place the bouquet in the makeshift vase.

"They're lovely. Thank you for bringing them," Joy said, feeling tears welling up again. Stupid hormones. "You've been my only visitor."

He frowned. "Is there anyone I can call for you?"

Joy shook her head, feeling a sudden fear grip her. "No! I mean, thank you, but since my husband died it's just me, and now, Katie. When Great Aunt Lil's lawyers finally located me in Denver and told me about the ranch, I decided to make a new beginning for us here in San Angelo." A safe place to escape my in-laws, she added silently.

Chance shifted his stance, then moved closer to the bed. "Look, Mrs. Spencer—"

"If I'm going to call you Chance then I think you can call me Joy."

Chance frowned. He hadn't meant to get too familiar with this woman. He came here to convince her that turning the Kirby Ranch into a profitable operation would cost a lot of money and take time, not to mention all the hard work. And it would be impossible for her to handle it on her own. After all, she was a city woman.

"Look, Joy, you probably didn't get much of a look at the property you inherited, but your aunt hadn't been running cattle for a long time. Maybe five years or so. It won't be easy getting things going again. There's been rain this past week, but we're still in a drought. The house is in pretty good shape but...."

"I don't care about the land, Mr. Randell."

"Chance," he corrected her.

"As I said, Chance, I'm not planning on raising cattle. Right now my main concern is the house. The Kirby Ranch is going to be my home now."

"So, you're not planning on running a herd?"

She shook her head, and Chance felt a weight lift from his shoulders. "I'm not a rancher," she said. "But I had thought about harvesting my aunt's pecan orchard and maybe putting in a vegetable garden." She picked at the bed linen. "But believe me, Katie and I plan on staying."

"Then you won't be offended if I offer to take the place off your hands." Chance began to pace the small area, then stopped and looked at her. "And at a fair price," he said. "Then you can move into town and take care of your daughter."

Joy couldn't believe the gall of this man. He wasn't listening to her. Most of her life, she'd moved from place to place. Since her parents' divorce, she hadn't had a permanent home for any length of time. Her short marriage to Blake had been as close as she'd gotten. But her father's aunt had left him a cattle ranch, and Joy was his only heir. She'd gladly taken Lil's place no matter what condition it was in. The ranch had been in her family for generations, and it would be Katie's one day. Most importantly, Joy desperately needed somewhere for herself and her baby to live, somewhere far away from the Spencers. Far away from any threat to her daughter.

Now, she had this big cowboy trying to get his hands on it. Well, no one was going to take her home away from her.

"I'm very capable of taking care of my daughter, Mr. Randell, we *are* going to live at the ranch."

He didn't look happy. "Fine, suit yourself," he finally said, then mumbled something about stubborn females as he jammed his cowboy hat on his head and stalked out.

"Thank you for the flowers," Joy called after him, wishing she hadn't just lost the only friend she'd made in town.

Chance parked his truck next to the barn, got out and slammed the door. His mood hadn't improved in the slightest during the twenty-minute drive home from the hospital. He marched across the gravel drive to the yard, then up the walk to the back porch of the large, two-story house he'd lived in for the past twenty-plus years.

That sure as hell didn't go well, he thought about

his talk with Joy Spencer. She'd rejected his offer fast. He couldn't help but wonder why. He didn't buy her story about the ranch being a family home. As far as he knew, she'd never once visited Lillian Kirby.

He thought back to his recent talk with Mrs. Spencer, remembering her elusive sapphire eyes. She had a secret. He couldn't hold that against her. People had a right to start over without everyone nosing into their business.

But there was no law that said he couldn't try again to buy her land. And he wasn't giving up. He jerked open the screen door and stepped into the utility room, jammed his hat on the peg and walked into the kitchen. The sunny yellow walls and biscuit-colored tile kept the room bright even at night. He glanced toward the double-door refrigerator. Hank was staring inside.

"What you lookin' for?" Chance asked.

"Something I'll never find as long as Ella works here. A decent meal."

In spite of his mood, Chance found himself smiling. The feud between Hank and the housekeeper had been going on for years. "Why don't you just fire her?" he asked for the hundredth time.

The older man stretched to his full six feet in height. Even in his mid sixties, Hank's back was ramrod straight, and his white hair was thick and wavy. Although his face was lined from years in the sun and showed his age, Hank Barrett could still outwork most men. He was a gruff man, but underneath he had a kind heart. How many men would have taken in three boys and given them a home?

"Who'd hire her?" he said. "She's too old to start

over. Besides, I guess I'm used to her ways. How long before she gets back from her sister's anyway?''

"Tomorrow," Chance answered. "You should have gotten a temporary cook in here to help. The hands haven't been too crazy about cooking their own meals."

"Well, dagnabbit," Hank said as he slammed the refrigerator door. "You'd think at least one of the men I hired could throw together a decent supper."

Chance grinned. "I take it it's your turn to feed us tonight."

Hank made a rude comment.

"Hey, we used to get into trouble for that kind of language." Chance couldn't help but think back to his adolescent days when he thought cursing made him seem tough. "You used to make me muck out stalls every time you caught me swearing, and I had to muck out more when Cade and Travis cursed."

"It was only fair, they learned that nasty talk from you."

Hank exchanged a sad glance with him. No doubt he was thinking about the two absent boys. "Sure would be nice if we got to see them once in awhile."

"Yeah, that would be nice." Chance would like to have them closer to home, but he couldn't ask Cade and Travis to give up the lives they'd made for themselves elsewhere. His brothers hadn't chosen ranching and that was all Chance had ever wanted to do.

From the time he had set foot on the Circle B at fourteen, he'd known he'd do anything to stay. He'd ended up helping his younger brothers with their chores just so Hank wouldn't turn them over to child services. He'd do whatever he had to so the Randell boys wouldn't be separated. Funny, but years later that's how it had turned out—Cade was in Chicago and Travis was in Houston.

"Maybe they'll surprise us and come for a visit this summer," Chance said.

"Sure. But I won't hold my breath." Hank walked to the pantry, then came out with three large cans of chili.

Chance thought that he should call Cade and Travis and see if he could coax them home to surprise Hank.

"How did your talk with Lil's niece go?" Hank asked as he worked the can opener.

Chance muffled a groan thinking about another night of heartburn. He went to the refrigerator and pulled out bacon and eggs. "Not good. She hasn't changed her mind. She's determined to move in."

The older man raised an eyebrow. "Sounds like she's inherited a little of Lil's stubbornness."

Chance didn't like the comparison. "It's foolhardy to move with a new baby into a place that's been deserted for nearly a year."

"Look, son, I know you're disappointed not to get the place, but the woman has a right to—"

Chance held up a hand. He didn't want to hear about right. "It's just a temporary setback. Joy Spencer will change her mind. She'll never survive."

"That's out of our hands. Besides, when Ella returns tomorrow and gets wind of the new neighbor, she'll be over there with her broom and bucket, cleaning. Maybe you should go over first and check out the place. Clear out anything that might have taken up residence."

Chance pulled out a skillet and set it on the front burner of the stainless-steel stove. He would do it, but he didn't have to like it. How was he supposed to feel, seeing her move into *his* place? All at once he remembered the tiny baby he'd seen in the nursery and knew he would make an effort. He'd had a taste of what it was like to be homeless.

"There isn't any rain in the forecast for the next week. I'll make sure all the windows get opened, and the place airs out. All that dust wouldn't be good for a baby."

"That little one got to ya, huh?" Hank's expression turned sad. "They used to get to Mae, too." Chance had never known Hank's wife; she'd died a few years before he and his brothers came to live at the ranch. But he remembered how lonely Hank looked whenever he talked about his Mae.

Chance placed strips of bacon in the cast-iron skillet. "I'm tryin' to do the right thing. She's gonna be our neighbor." He hoped it wouldn't be for too long, because he was also going to do everything possible to convince her to sell out to him.

The old man had a sober look on his face. "You say this woman is widowed?"

Chance nodded. "Says she has no family, just her daughter."

"By all means, you should do the right thing."

Chance ignored Hank's comment, telling himself he'd do as much for any neighbor. "I plan to."

Hank's tired hazel eyes lit up. "Hey, you think this Joy Spencer can cook?"

Two days later, Joy was more than ready to leave the hospital. On her tight budget she couldn't afford to stay any longer. She didn't have health insurance. There was the life insurance money she'd received after Blake's death, but that was all she had until she got on her feet and made a living off the ranch.

"Looks like you're ready to go."

Joy swung around at the sound of Chance Randell's voice. The tall man looked the part of a cowboy. His jeans appeared new and his light blue shirt was lightly starched, the sleeves rolled up past his elbows. His black, tooled boots shone, and he carried a straw Stetson in his broad hand.

Realizing that she was enjoying the view far too much, Joy redirected her attention to his face. "What are you doing here?"

"I'm taking you and the baby home," he said matter-of-factly.

"But...but you don't need to," Joy said, then realized her car was at the ranch, a good fifteen miles out of town. So it seemed Chance Randell was coming to her rescue again. She remembered how soothing he'd been to her in her time of need. But that was before. She couldn't forget he wanted to buy her out.

"Look, I'm just making sure you and...Katie, is it?"

Joy nodded.

"That you and Katie make it home okay. If Ella were here, she'd tell you to take it easy."

"Ella. Is she your wife?"

A half smile tugged at his mouth. "I'm not married. Ella is the cook and housekeeper at the Circle B." He raised a hand. "And I don't know how it is where you come from, but in Texas we help our neighbors."

He was right, she was too suspicious of his motives. "I'm sorry. Thank you, Chance, I'd really appreciate a lift to the ranch." She folded her arms over her tender breasts. "Tell me, do you spend all your free time rescuing women?"

"I assure you, I have plenty to keep me busy." His piercing gray eyes held hers. "But I couldn't sleep nights if I didn't make sure you and the little one get settled."

Joy knew he was right. She had a baby to think about. Katie deserved the best, the best from her mother. "Okay, but I'm going to pay you back for your kindness."

He pushed the wheelchair up to her. "I'm sure you will."

Chance watched as Joy nodded and went to finish packing up her things. Then the baby was brought in.

"Here you are, Katie," the nurse said as she laid the tiny bundle on the bed. "Your mommy and daddy are going to take you home," the young woman crooned to the infant. She looked up at Joy. "She is so adorable, we really hate to give her up. You and your husband are so lucky."

Joy glanced at Chance, and his stomach tightened at the thought of someone as beautiful as Joy Spencer being his. And a child... A yearning hit him like a rock to the gut.

"Yes, we are," Joy said. The nurse checked the wristbands on mother and daughter, then left. Avoiding his gaze, Joy tried to explain. "Sorry, it was just easier not to go through the whole long story."

"No problem," he grumbled, then glanced down at the baby who had stolen his heart the second he'd held her. "It's the closest I'll come to having a kid."

"You never know, Chance. Life is full of surprises." Joy picked up her child, then took a seat in the wheelchair. "C'mon, Katie, let's go to our new home."

Chance stared at Joy for a long time, thinking about his life and all that the name Randell had cost him. Nice women had stayed clear of the likes of him.

But since he'd first found Joy Spencer in the barn, he'd been drawn to her. Without question, she'd trusted him to deliver her baby. He glanced at the infant in her arms and his chest tightened. A yearning stirred deep inside him, making him want things he couldn't afford to want.

He quickly shook away the thought. He had to stay focused. He needed to convince Joy Spencer to sell him her land. And the sooner she left, the better.

Chapter Three

Carrying Katie Rose, Joy walked through the front door of the Kirby house. She glanced around with a gasp. She couldn't believe this was the same house she'd briefly walked through two days ago.

From the floors to the windows, everything sparkled. In the living room, the sheets had been removed from the furniture, the cobwebs were gone. The scent of lemon teased her nose as she noticed the high gloss on the tables and hardwood floors.

"Oh, my, the cleaning fairies must have been here," she whispered, amazed at the transformation.

Chance came in behind her, toting baby supplies the hospital sent home with all new mothers. "Ella, our housekeeper, rounded up some of the women from the local church to help get the house ready for you."

"They sure worked fast." Joy eyed him closely, wondering if he'd put in a few hours himself.

"Well, once word got around, everyone was curious about the new neighbor." His expression was impassive. "Especially with you just having had a baby. The ladies also did some baking, and stocked the kitchen with a few staples, just until you can get to the grocery store on your own."

Joy felt tears well up. "But they don't even know me."

"You're Lil Kirby's niece," he said. "Your aunt was well liked around here."

"I guess so." Joy wiped away a tear, remembering she had only met her great-aunt once when she was a child. Back when her parents had still been married, and Joy had had a family.

"You okay?" Chance asked.

She sniffed and nodded, suddenly feeling tired. "Just my silly hormones."

"You need to rest. You had a baby less than forty-eight hours ago."

Joy caught his silver-eyed gaze. Was it only two days ago that this man had helped her give birth to Katie? If it hadn't been for his coming to her rescue, she might not be bringing her daughter home today. The thought terrified her. "Did I ever thank you for all your help?"

"Too many times," he said. "You need to rest. Wait here, I'll take the baby upstairs, then come back for you."

Before Joy could reply, Chance took the carrier from Joy and climbed the steps to the second floor, returning seconds later.

"Your turn," he said as he suddenly swung her up in his arms.

"Wait, you can't carry me. I'm too heavy." Feeling herself blush, she could only loop her arms around his neck, immediately feeling his muscles flex under his skin.

"You're not heavy. Besides, you look about as shaky as a new colt. Right now you need to save your strength so you can take care of Katie. I have orders from both the doctor and Ella to make sure you get some rest. And I don't mess around when Ella gives orders."

Joy opened her mouth, but didn't know how to answer him. He was right, she needed to take care of herself. She was all Katie had. Her body was still sore, and her daughter would soon be awake and wanting to be fed.

But Joy couldn't let this big, charge-into-her-life cowboy take over. She had to stand on her own. Soon. But right now, it felt too nice to let someone else handle things.

Chance reached the top step without even breathing hard. "I figured since this was the largest room," he said, "you'd want to move in here." He carried her down the hall and into the master bedroom. He set her down beside a wrought-iron bed. Next to that was a bassinet. Joy glanced inside and saw Katie sleeping.

"I suggest you take advantage of this quiet time and get some rest." Chance walked to the door. "I'll check in on you later." He left, closing the door behind him.

Joy glanced around the recently cleaned bedroom. The floral wallpaper was old and faded. The sheer curtains in the window had seen better days as had the rug that covered most of the floor. The bassinet was wicker and probably fifty years old. Joy ran her hand over the freshly laundered white eyelet skirt with loving hands as her beautiful daughter slept peacefully in her new bed. "She looks like you, Blake. She has your eyes," she whispered. Sadness nearly overtook her as she thought of her husband not seeing his child grow up; of Katie not having a father around. But Joy knew one thing for sure. She was going to give her daughter a home and plenty of love.

Now she just had to figure out how she was going to make a living on a cattle ranch.

Two hours later, with orders from Ella to check on the new mother, Chance walked through the back door and into the kitchen. The house was silent, which probably meant that mother and baby were still napping. But they would be hungry soon.

He went to the ancient refrigerator and pulled out a container of homemade chicken soup one of the ladies had made. He poured the liquid into a pan and began heating it up on the small stove. Taking a tray from the pantry, he searched for a bowl in the cupboard, discovering several doors and drawers that needed fixing. The flooring was pretty worn, but it would hold for a while.

He made a mental note of the repairs and wondered when Joy would realize that the ranch was too much for her and sell it to him. She wasn't going to want to take on running a ranch when she had a baby to care for. If she needed to stay in San Angelo, she could buy a house in town.

He placed the bowl of soup on the tray, along with crackers and a glass of milk and headed upstairs. On the way he glanced around the large house, seeing some other things that needed attention. Nothing he couldn't handle. But when he bought the ranch, they were all going to have to wait, because his first concern would be the grazing land and enlarging the herd.

He pushed open the partly closed door, looked up and froze at the sight before him. Joy was on the bed, but she was awake with her baby suckling at her breast.

He felt the heat rush through his body to his face. "Uh... I'm sorry... I didn't know...."

Joy glanced up and saw a shocked Chance staring at her. She quickly pulled a receiving blanket over her shoulder, covering herself. "Chance, I didn't hear you come in," she said, trying to distract from the awkward moment.

"Ella said you needed something to eat." He walked into the room, set the tray on the other side of the bed, then started backing up toward the door. "Were you able to get any rest?"

"Yes, I slept until about fifteen minutes ago." She glanced down at her daughter. "I guess we were both tired."

He kept staring at her, then finally spoke, "Well, I should get back to my chores. Is there anything you need before I go?"

"No, you've done so much already. I think I can handle things. Thanks for the soup. I was getting a little hungry."

He leaned against the door frame, his large body taking up most of the space. "It's important you keep up your strength."

"I know."

"Oh, I called the phone company. They'll be out in the morning. Until then..." He pulled a small cellular phone from his pocket and came back across the room.

"Use this. Press one, then Send, and you'll get the Circle B."

Joy was touched by his concern. "Thank you again." Just then Katie started to fuss.

Chance jumped. "I'll be going," he said. "I'll check in later." And he was out the door.

Joy lifted her tiny daughter to her shoulder and began patting her back. "Well, sweetheart, like it or not, looks like we got ourselves a big cowboy looking out for us." But for how long? she wondered, knowing the ranch was what he really wanted.

The next morning, Katie was awake at six. She'd slept four straight hours. After feeding her, Joy tried her hand at the first bath. Her daughter wasn't ready to be submerged in water, but a sponge bath was due.

Joy loved the experience. All the talking and cooing to the baby and that clean powdery smell was so intoxicating. Soon Katie was worn out and went back to sleep. A few minutes to herself, Joy thought. Baby monitor in hand and last night's bowl of soup a distant memory, she headed downstairs in search of food. She started for the kitchen, and the aroma of bacon assaulted her nose. She thought she was dreaming, until she found Chance standing at her stove.

Looking as if he'd recently showered and shaved, he wore butt-hugging jeans and a blue western shirt over broad shoulders. His sandy hair was lying across his forehead, and she could see the mark of his hat just above his ears.

Realizing what she was doing, she shook her head and stiffened. Didn't this man have anything else to do? Was he here to badger her again about selling her ranch?

"Aren't your cows feeling neglected? I mean I don't want to keep you from your job." Pulling together her robe, she ran her fingers through her hair. She looked a mess.

"I was out there at five," he said as he glanced over his shoulder. "Everything's fine. In fact we have five new calves."

"Oh, really?" she said, finding she was actually interested in the workings of the ranch. "I bet they're cute."

"Cute? I don't think about calves that way. It's not wise to get attached to animals who are going to be sold at market."

"I guess you're right." She went to the coffee-maker, unable to resist the smell of the fresh brew. The doctor had assured her one cup a day wouldn't hurt the baby. Taking a mug from the cabinet, she poured herself some.

"How do you like your eggs?" he asked.

"Look, I appreciate your help, but I don't need you to take care of me. I can fix my own breakfast."

"Never turn down a man wanting to cook for you." A woman's voice rang out from the pantry.

Joy watched as a tall, sturdily built woman with short gray hair walked to the table. She was dressed in dark jeans and a plaid shirt.

"Hi, I'm Ella, the Circle B's housekeeper. Sorry to intrude so early." She smiled at Joy. "We were hoping to have your breakfast ready before you came down."

Embarrassed, Joy held out her hand. "Hi, I'm Joy. It's nice to meet you. I'm the one who should be sorry. You and the other ladies have been so kind to me."

"But good intentions can be overwhelming," Ella said. "We'll leave."

"Oh, please stay," Joy insisted. "You haven't even seen the baby."

The older woman smiled. "Well, I wouldn't mind hanging around for a peek just in case she wakes up. And Chance here can finish your breakfast. Don't worry, he's a good cook, he learned long before he came to the Circle B, and before I could do any damage."

Joy smiled as soft cooing sounds came over the monitor.

Ella's eyes lit up. "You sit down and have your coffee and I'll go check on the baby."

Reluctantly Joy nodded and sat down at the table. She sipped her coffee and watched Chance work efficiently at the small stove that looked as if it had been purchased some time around the Second World War. "So your mom taught you how to cook?"

He shook his head. "Hardly. My mother died when I was young. My brothers and I pretty much had to fend for ourselves." He removed the bacon, then cracked an egg on the edge of the skillet and dropped it into the grease. "I figured if I wanted to eat, I'd better learn."

Joy shook her head. "I'm dreaming. A man who can cook."

He glanced at her again. "I didn't say I liked to do it on a regular basis, but I figured you needed something to eat."

"I'm feeling much better this morning. In fact, I just gave Katie a bath and plan on heading to the shower myself. Just as soon as I finish breakfast."

Chance scooped the eggs onto a plate and carried

it to table. "Then dig in." He returned with toast, then sat down with some coffee.

Joy started on the bacon. "You aren't having anything?"

"I ate hours ago." He took a sip from his mug.

She felt weird. Most of her life she'd had to fend for herself. Now she had a rugged cowboy who wouldn't go away. But she couldn't let him hang around. He was only being nice because he wanted her home. "Don't feel like you have to stay. Really, Chance, I appreciate everything, but I feel I've been taking you away from your work."

"It's not roundup yet, so I have the time. I understand if you want to be alone." He stood. "But you should have someone around for awhile. Your closest neighbor is five miles up the road. So if not me, let Ella stay, at least while you take a shower." He poured his coffee into the old chipped sink, and set his mug on the counter. "Don't be too proud to accept help." He walked to the door.

Joy felt like a heel. She almost called him back. But she couldn't. She had to do this on her own. She had to prove to herself and to the Spencers that she could raise her child. And having a man around only reminded her of what she'd lost and what she would never have again.

Someone who cared for her. Someone to love.

Chance rode Ace hard, all the way to the outskirts of the ranch to Mustang Valley. He needed to vent his frustration. As they came to the edge of the creek that ran through a grove of trees, he pulled on the reins to slow the animal. The horse danced along the shore, eager for a well-deserved drink.

Angry with himself, Chance climbed down and dropped the reins to the ground, knowing Ace would stay put. Pulling off his gloves, he crouched and cupped his hand in the water and drank until he'd cooled off some. But it didn't work and wouldn't any time soon. Not until he stopped seeing red. Every time he thought about Joy Spencer he saw red.

Then there was a whole slew of feelings she stirred in him. Just looking at her pretty face and her long blond hair wild and sassy, made desire surge through him. Damn, he couldn't think of her that way, she'd just had a baby. But his thoughts went to yesterday when he walked into the bedroom and found Joy nursing. The picture of the tiny infant suckling at her creamy breast had kept him tossing and turning all night.

With a string of curses, he marched to the shade tree and leaned against the huge oak. A breeze brushed his face as his gaze traveled over the lush valley, and calmness moved through him. Although the rain had been light this year, it had been enough to keep things growing. But was there enough grazing land to enlarge the herd? There could be if he could get the Kirby Ranch.

He pulled off his hat and smoothed back his damp hair. Closing his eyes, he tried to push away the fear that plagued him. Why couldn't he have this one thing? Why couldn't he have something that was his? Hadn't he worked hard enough? Hadn't he paid enough?

Suddenly ugly memories of his childhood surfaced. He'd never been able to put away the past. His life on the small family ranch; how his daddy tried to make

a go of it. He also remembered how many times Jack
Randell failed. Too many.

Even as a boy, Chance had known his dad had always looked for the easy way out. Hard work had been
foreign to him. He couldn't even keep the ranch that
he inherited from his daddy from going under.
Couldn't keep it long enough to hand it down to his
sons. With the drought and sinking cattle prices, Jack
ended up owing everyone. Then, while other ranchers
were selling off their herds, things were only getting
better for the Randells. But as the sheriff soon learned,
Jack had been rustling cattle.

At fourteen, Chance should have been able to look
up to his father, instead he felt nothing but shame. By
the time their daddy had been sentenced to prison, the
ranch was gone, and the three boys were on their own.
The brothers were shunned by everyone, and years
later, some people still couldn't forgive any Randell,
even if the sons had been innocent.

It had taken a long time, but Chance had built a
name for himself, a good name as a rancher and as a
horse breeder. But that didn't mean everyone had forgotten who his father was. They probably never
would.

Chance opened his eyes and looked toward the far
end of the valley. About fifty yards away, he spied the
familiar herd of mustangs. About a dozen of them
wandered cautiously toward the edge of the stream. A
mare guarded her new spring colt as the proud buckskin stallion led the group.

Most of the ponies were a mixed breed now, but
the Spanish bloodline was rich through these remain-
ing few. A lot of people thought the mustangs were a

nuisance, but Hank had taught Chance and his brothers to respect the animals.

Chance had always felt a connection to the horses. He loved to watch these wild creatures. How hard they fought to be free, and finally banded together to keep safe. This valley was a refuge for the mustangs, and a comforting reminder for him that it was home for all misfits, including him and his brothers.

He belonged here. This was where he felt at home. And with the Kirby Ranch he would be able to fulfill his dream of his own place. Now he just had to convince one stubborn city woman to sell.

Chapter Four

An hour later, after a leisurely shower, Joy felt much better. A little makeup helped hide the dark shadows under her eyes, but nothing could help her get into her pre-maternity clothes. She ended up putting on a loose gauzy skirt and an oversized blouse. She fed Katie again, then came downstairs to have some decaffeinated tea with Ella.

"You're going to like it here in San Angelo," the Circle B housekeeper said. "It's a nice area, and for the most part, good people. And don't hesitate to ask for help. At least until you get back on your feet. There's plenty of women around here who would love to get their hands on that precious baby upstairs."

Joy smiled. "Everyone has been so good to us." Her thoughts went to Chance Randell, wishing she hadn't been so rude to him. How could she have practically thrown him out? But his motives weren't completely generous. He wanted her ranch.

"Well, a woman alone has to be careful," Ella said, then took another sip of her tea.

"I thought you said I was safe here. Aunt Lillian lived alone here, and she was never bothered. Was she?"

Ella smiled. "Naw, but your Aunt Lil was an expert with a shotgun. And everyone around here knew it."

Joy shook her head. "I've never fired a gun. I don't much care for them."

"Well, you should learn, even if it's just to run off coyotes."

Joy's heart began to race. Coyotes! She was alone here and...with a baby. She remembered how pitch black it had been outside her window last night. Luckily, her aunt had installed security lights on the property, and Joy could see all the way to the barn.

"It's okay, Joy. Just stay in touch with your neighbors. We depend on each other a lot. And I suggest you get a dog. In fact, Betty Campbell's son's dog had a litter of pups over a month ago. They should be ready for homes."

"A dog?" She'd always wanted a dog when she was growing up, but her mother wouldn't let her have one because they'd lived in a apartment. Joy's interest was definitely piqued. "What kind of dog?" she asked.

"I hear they're a Labrador mix. Great dogs. Good around kids."

"You think I could buy one?"

Ella nodded. "And I bet it's at a price you can't pass up, too."

Joy didn't want Ella to know how uneasy she really felt. She was out of her element here. How could she handle everything: a baby, a dog, a ranch? And what if the Spencers found…?

No, she wasn't going to get discouraged. She pushed away the negative thoughts. The Spencers weren't going to find her. They hadn't any idea where she'd gone. Joy had been careful not to leave a trail. Only her friend Terri knew of her plans.

"I'll have Chance pick one out if you're interested," Ella said.

"What?" Joy asked, embarrassed she hadn't been listening.

"The puppy. Chance will make sure you get a good one."

"Oh, no, I don't want to put him to any trouble." She didn't need the man to do her any more favors.

Ella shook her head. "It's no problem. Chance deals with the Campbells all the time. He bred two of their mares."

Joy was surprised. "I thought he was in the cattle business."

"He is," Ella said. "But he's also been breeding and training quarter horses for several years now." The housekeeper cocked her head. "I guess it's no secret Chance hoped to buy this place."

Joy wasn't sure that she wanted to get into this. "I'm sorry…"

The older woman's hand covered Joy's. "It's okay, Joy. You and your baby have every right to be here. I know Chance is disappointed, but maybe something else will come up for him. He can take it. He's tough. He's had to be over the years to survive."

Joy didn't miss the flash of pain in Ella's eyes when she spoke of Chance. There was more to learn about that brooding cowboy. And it frightened her to realize how much she wanted to know about him.

Chance glanced from the road to the box on the truck seat. The chocolate and blond lab puppies were whining and scampering up the side, trying to escape their temporary home.

He reached over and stroked the animals. "Hang on, you guys. I'll get you a new home soon."

Yeah, thanks to Ella, he'd been elected deliveryman today. Did she think he had nothing else to do than run errands for Joy Spencer? Chance wiped his hand over his face and released a long sigh. What was wrong with him? He'd done the same for neighbors before.

He knew the truth was he was still ticked off because she had practically chased him away three days ago. Okay, he'd gotten the message loud and clear. She didn't want him around. So, what? He wasn't crazy about the idea of her being his neighbor, either.

He gripped the steering wheel tighter and blew out a long breath. "Stop beating a dead horse," he mumbled, hating the circumstances. "She's here. So get used to it."

He may have to live with it, but he didn't have to hang around. As soon as he dropped off the dog, he was out of there. He pulled off the highway and drove down the gravel road about another quarter mile until he came to the Kirby place. He pulled up next to the house and climbed out. Carrying the box, he walked to the back door and knocked.

Just give her the box and leave, he told himself. She wanted her privacy. Let her run the ranch. Let her see how hard things were, and maybe then she'd be more willing to sell. He'd give her two months.

Finally the door opened and Joy appeared. She was dressed in a pink blouse and some kind of black stretch pants. Her hair was pulled into a ponytail, and she was holding her crying daughter against her shoulder. Maybe screaming was a better description. Chance's attention went to Joy and stopped at the panic in her once-bright eyes.

"What's wrong?" He felt his own panic build. He came inside and set the box down in the mudroom.

"I don't know. Katie's been fussing since her two o'clock feeding. I've fed her and changed her, but she hasn't slept." Joy tucked a strand of hair behind her ear. "I don't know what to do."

Not stopping to ask permission, Chance took the baby from Joy. He managed to brace the squirming bundle against his shoulder and began talking to the infant. "What's wrong, little darlin'? You have a rough night?"

As if little Katie understood him, her cries softened and he continued to walk around the room, patting her back. After a few minutes she emitted a very unlady-like burp. Katie sobbed softly for a moment longer, then there was silence.

Joy felt the tears build in her eyes as she looked at the big cowboy holding her daughter. Why couldn't Katie have done that for her? Joy had been carrying her all night, worrying that she'd eaten something that didn't agree with her daughter.

Awkwardly, Chance put the sleeping baby in the carrier on the table, then he turned to Joy. "Hope she'll sleep for a while."

"Thank you."

"No problem." Suddenly the tenderness was gone as the familiar stony gaze appeared in his gray eyes. "What about you? When was the last time you ate?"

What was it about this man wanting to feed her? "Last night. And some toast this morning." She was capable of feeding herself.

Suddenly they were aware of a different whimpering sound coming from the back door. They both glanced over to the box on the porch. Chance retrieved the carton and brought it into the kitchen.

Joy peeked inside at the two lively pups. "Oh, they're so cute." She reached in and both animals began licking her hand. She picked up the brown one, but the yellow dog began to whine. So Joy scooped them both up. Big mistake. They were all over her, and she ended up sitting down on the floor, allowing them to have their way with her. It wasn't until she discovered Chance had been watching her antics that she sobered.

"Which one is my dog?"

"You tell me," Chance said, his arms folded over his chest. "They were the last two of the litter."

"You mean I have to choose?" She eyed the pair, then looked at him. "Which do you think?"

He knelt down beside her and reached for the blond dog, scooping her up in his large hand. "This little lady has clear eyes. She's got a good disposition, too." He set her down, then held up the brown one. "This girl is the runt of the litter. Out of the two, the blonde will probably be a prettier dog, but sometimes the littlest works the hardest to please and is the most loyal." His eyes locked with Joy's, and she felt her pulse take off.

Whoa, where did that come from? She glanced

away. "Well, I can't decide. I've fallen in love with both. Is it possible for me to have them both?"

He didn't even blink, as if he'd known that was what she would do. "They're going to eat a lot."

She shrugged. The man was so argumentative. "So, I'll buy more dog food."

A hint of a smile teased his mouth. "You'll need a bigger box."

"I have plenty upstairs."

He nodded. "Then I'll bring the dog food in from my truck." He stood, and she couldn't help but watch the cowboy in the faded jeans walk away. Nice rear end, she thought, her gaze continuing up the tan western shirt covering his broad back and wide shoulders. Just then he turned around. Heat shot to her face as a blush colored her cheeks.

He looked at her curiously. "You want the food on the porch or in the barn?"

"Here. I'll keep them on the porch for now."

He nodded, then turned and disappeared outside. Joy sighed in relief and put the puppies back in the box. She had to stop looking at the man as if he were chocolate fudge. Breast-feeding, she knew she couldn't have any chocolate for a while…or ever for that matter.

She stood and went to the kitchen table to check on Katie. Her tiny daughter was still sleeping peacefully in her carrier.

"Looks like we're getting settled in, sweetie. Just like I promised. Now we've got two more to add to our family." Joy glanced down at the animals who'd decided there had been too much excitement and curled up together, their eyes drooping shut.

"I guess all we need now is to decide on names.

She thought a minute. "How about Ginger, for the brown one? And Sunny, for the yellow one."

The door opened again, and the sound of a large bag being dropped got Joy's attention.

"So, you named them yet?"

Joy smiled proudly. "Yup. Ginger and Sunny are the new members of the Spencer family."

Chance murmured something about a house full of women, turned and left.

Joy called out "thank you" as she watched him leave, then heard the slam of the screen door. She regretted not allowing herself to be friendlier to the man who had helped her once again. Maybe she should have invited him to stay, offered him something to drink. Why was it every time the man was around her she couldn't seem to think straight? Was it only because she couldn't trust his motives? Chance wanted her to fail so he could take away everything she'd always wanted. No, this was the safest way. She needed a home to insure she didn't lose Katie. And she'd do anything to keep her daughter.

Angry, Chance drove down the highway faster than usual. Every time he was around Joy Spencer he let her get under his skin. Friendly one minute, then cold and distant the next, she'd made it clear she didn't want him there.

"I sure as hell don't need the headache she gives me," he grumbled, but soon remembered holding Katie, the sweet bundle that managed to turn his insides to mush. He also recalled the frightened look in Joy's blue eyes when she'd opened the door to him. Something was terribly wrong, and there wasn't anyone around to help. What would she do? Who would she have to help her? Stop it, he told himself. He couldn't keep being her rescuer, especially when she didn't want to be rescued. Well, from now on, Ella could be the good neighbor.

Chance pulled onto the gravel road that led to the Circle B and parked next to the horse barn. The large white structure was only ten years old. Hank had had the horse barn constructed when Chance began breeding quarter horses. Hank's faith had always amazed Chance. It was the reason he'd been able to build quite a reputation with his horses. He glanced at the half-dozen pregnant mares lazily moving around the corral. On the other side were two ranch hands working colts at different stages of their training. He felt a surge of pride in what he'd accomplished. Some people around the area might not forget he was a Randell, but they trusted his ability with animals. He could handle it...for now.

So why did he want more from Joy Spencer?

At six that evening, Chance walked into the house from the barn. He washed up at the sink in the utility room, then came into the large kitchen to find Ella busy making supper.

She glanced over her shoulder. "You're later than usual tonight."

"Guess I lost track of time."

The tall woman walked across the large kitchen and touched his forehead. "No fever. There must have been something mighty special to keep you from a meal."

Chance ignored Ella's teasing and went to the refrigerator. He pulled out a pitcher of ice tea, poured himself a glass, and, leaning against the counter, took a long drink. "If you hadn't sent me all over the county running errands, maybe I could have gotten my chores done in time."

A smile showed off the tiny lines around Ella's eyes. "So you took the puppy over to Joy."

"The Campbells had two left. She ended up keeping them both."

"You don't say." Ella shrugged. "Well, I'm not surprised. She seems determined to fill up that big place. And in a few months they'll be good watchdogs."

"Until then she's got three babies to take care of," Chance said. "Not to mention a ranch." The woman was taking on a lot.

"Then I guess the neighbors are going to have to pitch in."

"And do what? Help change diapers?"

"Wouldn't hurt to learn," Ella said as she carried a large pot roast to the table. "Every new mother needs help."

"She needed it today." Chance set his glass in front of his usual seat around the long table. "When I arrived the little one was screaming her head off."

"Oh, no. Was something wrong?"

"Just a stomachache." He couldn't stop remembering how the baby felt in his arms. She was so little…so fragile.

"I should go by tomorrow and see if she needs anything," Ella said.

"Good idea. I'll be driving to Midland to pick up a mare."

"Will you be back in time for supper?"

"Not sure." Chance usually stayed over in Midland, mainly to spend time with Nita Cruz, a good-looking woman he'd met at a cattle auction about three years ago. From the beginning it had been a "no-strings" arrangement. When Chance made it to town every few months they both enjoyed renewing the…relationship.

Suddenly his thoughts flashed to the blue-eyed woman who had been disrupting his life for the past week. He couldn't seem to keep her at a distance. He told himself that it was because she had something he wanted. The ranch. But he knew that every time he was around her, she had him feeling things he had no business feeling. Like the charge of awareness he'd felt watching her romp around on the kitchen floor with the puppies. All he could think about was tangling his hands in her wild curls, pulling her close so he could finally get a taste of her tempting mouth.

He quickly shook away the direction his thoughts were going. Damn. He definitely needed a few days in Midland.

Hank walked into the kitchen and greeted Ella, then glanced at Chance. "How's the mare doin'?"

He shrugged as he thought about his prize bay horse, Sweet Lady Grey, and how important her first foal was. "Nothing yet. Sweetness is taking her time. I have Carlos watching her closely. If anything happens he'll call me."

"What did Doc Jenkins say?"

"He feels she'll go another few days, and we should just let nature take its course."

Hank chuckled as he washed up in the sink. "Easy for him to say. He doesn't have any money riding on this filly's first colt."

Chance listened to Hank's words and began to worry. There *was* a lot riding on this foal. If everything went well, this foal's impressive bloodline would sure help his breeding business. "Maybe I shouldn't go to Midland."

"No, son, you go on. You can't let this deal slip by, either. Word is getting around about your horses. The Henderson Ranch could do a lot for you."

Ella set a big bowl of green beans on the table. "Chance just thinks he's the expert on delivering babies around here," the housekeeper teased.

Hank laughed as he sat down at the head of the table. "I heard Carlos say that since you're so experienced now, your name and number are going up as next to call after the midwife."

Chance accepted the good-natured ribbing. He knew it was done with love; over the years he'd had enough of the other kind to know the difference. "Well, if I'm needed, I'll go." He dished some pot roast onto his plate.

He felt Ella's hand on his arm. "You did a wonderful thing. I hate to think what would have happened if Joy had been alone. You should be proud of yourself, Chance Randell, for helping that precious baby into the world."

He should be used to Ella's praise by now. For nearly twenty years, she'd always been there for him and his brothers. She'd been more than the Circle B's housekeeper; she'd been the mother he'd never had. The one person who'd seen him at his most stubborn and most vulnerable. Ella and Hank had been the only two people he'd allowed to see his weaknesses. Not even his brothers knew their older brother was ever anything but in control.

It had taken years to build a wall of protection for himself, and now one blue-eyed city woman was dangerously close to tearing it down. He couldn't let that happen.

"Well, aren't you in a good mood this morning?" Joy said as she finished dressing Katie in a clean gown. After wrapping her in a receiving blanket, Joy picked up the freshly bathed baby. "Oh, you smell so good."

Her daughter cooed.

"Well, you do." She kissed her cheek, and they headed down the steps. "And you know what else? You're just the prettiest baby in the whole wide world." She thought of Blake and a twinge of sadness gripped her. "You look like your daddy."

In the kitchen, Joy placed her daughter in the carrier on the scarred maple table. "Now, if you sit here and let your mama eat then my day would start off perfect." Once again the baby puckered up her lips and gurgled.

Joy had some toast and a half cup of coffee, then went to the porch and checked on her new charges. "How are my other girls today?" she asked and was answered by both puppies whining and scampering against the side of the box.

After feeding Ginger and Sunny some breakfast, she took the dogs outside and let them run around the yard. Then she brought Katie's carrier outside so they both could enjoy the warm spring day and watch Ginger's and Sunny's antics in the tall grass.

With a long sigh, Joy took a seat on the faded yellow metal glider. Placing her daughter at her feet, she leaned back and looked off through the grove of pecan trees to the thick green grass that covered the rolling hillsides. She glanced up at the endless blue sky and was amazed at the rich hue. Back in Denver the horizon had been clouded by the high-rises and pollution. Not here. She drew a deep breath of the sweet-smelling air. Excitement raced through her as she realized she could only find perfection in her new home.

"Well, how do you like it so far, Katie?"

Her daughter's arms waved in the air.

"It's a little overwhelming, isn't it? And it's all ours. Someday you're going to appreciate having a big yard." Joy leaned over and touched her daughter's rosy cheek, feeling such overwhelming love it brought tears to her eyes. "And one day maybe your own pony. Of course, you'll have to learn to ride. I'll have to learn to ride," she murmured as her thoughts turned to her brooding neighbor. She doubted Chance Randell would be willing to give her lessons. He was just waiting for her to give up, turn tail and run back to Denver. "Well, he can just wait, because we aren't going anywhere, are we?" Katie Rose gave her a big yawn. She was here to stay.

Joy gathered up all her girls and returned to the house. She had a lot to do today and no time to waste. She put the baby down for her nap and began wandering through the rest of the upstairs. It didn't taken long to see that Great Aunt Lillian hadn't done much to the house in a while, but there was nothing major needing to be done. All the plumbing and electricity seemed to work fine. But a fresh coat of paint and some new wallpaper would do wonders.

By the time Joy had investigated the downstairs, her excitement had grown, and she decided to call her friend, Terri. She hadn't even had a chance to let her know about the baby.

Joy picked up the phone and began to dial. She

owed Terri a lot. Her friend was the one who'd helped her get away, who'd helped her pack up her meager belongs and literally sneak off into the night.

After the second ring her friend's familiar voice came on the line. "Hi Terri, it's me—"

"Oh, Mary!" Terri interrupted. "Oh, it's been so long. Look, I can't talk right now, but can you call me back in about thirty minutes? Bye."

Then there was a click and a dial tone. Something was wrong, and Joy bet the Spencers were behind it.

Holding out for the next half hour was rough, but finally Joy picked up the phone. She punched out the numbers and her friend answered.

"Oh, Joy. I'm so glad you called me back."

"Terri, what's going on?"

"The Spencers were here. Joy, they're not happy."

"You didn't tell them anything, did you?"

"Of course not," Terri said. "But I've never seen anyone so angry as Mr. Spencer. And Mrs. Spencer is desperate to find you."

Joy's heart pounded in fear. She knew what a chance she'd taken crossing James Spencer. "Of course. They want my baby."

"And I don't think they're going to stop until they find you. They hired a private investigator." Terri assured her of what she already knew. "Joy, I've been so worried with you being pregnant and driving around Texas."

"Well, you don't have to worry any more. I've had my baby already. A little girl, Katie Rose."

"Oh, Joy. I wish I could have been there. Did you have a rough time?"

"You have no idea. But thanks to a neighborly cowboy we're both doing fine." Joy's thoughts went back just a week to the scene in the barn, Chance's calming words helping her to bring her daughter into the world. Now Katie was more vulnerable than before. Joy couldn't let the Spencers find her.

"Terri, do you think Blake's parents have any idea where I am?"

"No, but it's only a matter of time. Joy, why don't you come home here and fight them? They can't take your child away."

"I can't, Terri. James Spencer is a determined man. He never wanted me to marry his son to begin with. Do you think he'll allow me to raise his only grandchild?" A shiver raced through Joy. She was a single parent now. "I can't risk it. I'm staying here.... This is our home now." The only real home Joy had ever had. "With Blake's insurance and my aunt's money, I can get by for a while."

"You can always do medical transcripts there and work right out of the house."

Joy thought about the laptop computer she'd brought with her. "I know, but right now I want to concentrate on being Katie's mom."

"Oh, I bet she's adorable. Send me a picture when you get a chance."

"Oh, gosh, I hadn't even thought about pictures." That's because Joy hadn't anyone, besides Terri, to send them to.

"Well, get busy, I want to get a look at my goddaughter. It's going to be a while before I can come for a visit."

"Terri, you know you're welcome to come and live with Katie and me. This house is plenty big enough."

"Thanks, I'll think about it. Now give me a number so I can call you."

Joy recited the number of the ranch house then said goodbye. She let her tears fall as she ran upstairs to the nursery. She stood next to the bassinet and watched tiny Katie sleeping so peacefully.

Oh, God. She couldn't let James and Margaret Spencer take her baby. But she knew that with their wealth they also had power, especially in Denver. And no doubt they could afford to give Katie material things. Too bad they didn't know how to love. Their own child had been shunned by his father because he refused to bend to his will. James Spencer wanted his son to follow in his footsteps. But gentle, loving Blake could never be the ruthless businessman his father was. The last tie with the Spencer family had been broken when their son had defiantly married a girl who hadn't come from an acceptable family, but she and Blake had had so much more: love.

Joy tucked the blanket over her daughter. "And you're going to have your mother's love, sweetie. Always," she managed to get the words past the tears in her throat. She and Katie were a family now. And no one was going to take her child away. She'd do anything to keep that from happening. Anything.

Even if it meant she had find a father for Katie...and marry him.

Chapter Five

"**A**re you sure, Mr. Keefer?" Joy asked as she sat perched on the edge of the chintz-covered chair in the lawyer's office. Her shoes were nearly buried in the plush earth-toned carpet.

She really couldn't afford a lawyer, but she also couldn't afford not to consult one. If the Spencers were coming after her she needed the best, and Michael F. Keefer specialized in custody cases.

"As sure as I can be, Mrs. Spencer," the forty-something lawyer said. "In my experience, a judge usually doesn't take a child away from her mother without good reason."

Joy wished his answer made her feel better. But when it came to dealing with the Spencers, she would never be confident. James Spencer was used to getting what he wanted, one way or the other. And somehow, she had to stop him from winning now.

"If you're holding anything back about your past, Mrs. Spencer, it's imperative I know now."

Joy shook her head. "No, Mr. Keefer, Blake and I met in college. Before that, I had never had a long-term boyfriend." She knew what he wanted to know. Would some man come out of the woodwork to tell sordid stories about her past? "My husband was my only lover."

Mr. Keefer smiled and nodded.

Joy felt a blush creeping up her neck and tried to concentrate on Katie, sound asleep in her carrier. She hated the thought of having her personal life exposed in court. "What do we do now?" she asked.

"Nothing. If the Spencers call or pay you a visit, I want to know about it. But they'll have to make the first move."

"Do I have to let them know where I am?"

He shook his head. "No. As of now, they have limited rights to their grandchild. You have every right to keep Katie away from any disturbing influences."

Joy clasped her trembling hands, wishing his words gave her more comfort. "Is there a problem because I'm a single mother? I mean, could the judge decide that a two-parent home would be better for my baby?"

Michael Keefer stood and came around the desk. "Two parents would be the best situation, but a lot of single parents are raising kids today."

Joy wanted every advantage to ensure her rights to Katie. "But if I were to get married again and provide a father for my daughter...I mean, wouldn't that be more favorable for me?"

The lawyer's eyes narrowed as he studied her. "I would suggest if there *is* a man in your life that you do not live together without marriage."

"Yes, of course, that would be the only way," she murmured almost to herself. She'd sworn she'd never

marry again. She could never love anyone except
Blake. But she was fighting for the most important
thing in her life. Her daughter. She had a lot to think
about. "Well, thank you, Mr. Keefer." She stood and
took the handle of Katie's carrier. "You've been very
helpful."

He shook her hand. "Please, call me if you need
anything, or if the Spencers contact you."

She nodded and walked out the door, praying that
she wouldn't be found. But knowing James and Margaret Spencer, it was only a matter of time. And that
terrified her.

Joy stepped into the elevator and pushed the button
to the lobby. She had to do something more to protect
her baby. She looked down at the tiny sleeping baby.
The love she felt for her daughter was overwhelming,
and she'd do anything to keep her promise to give her
a safe and loving home. Joy could give her that at the
ranch. Suddenly a fierce protectiveness washed over
her. Katie Rose was depending on her mother, and she
wouldn't let her down, no matter what she had to do.

Joy thought of Chance Randell. He hadn't come by
for a few days. Had he changed his mind about wanting the ranch? She prayed not. She had an offer for
him she hoped he couldn't turn down.

The next afternoon, Joy paced the kitchen, adding
more mileage to the already-worn flooring. She was
nervous and hadn't been able to sit still, hoping that
the pacing would help burn energy. It hadn't. She
walked into the hall and looked in the long mirror on
the inside of the closet door, checking her appearance.
She'd pulled her hair back with clips, letting it fall to
her shoulders in curls. She'd put on her favorite black

T-shirt and tucked it into a black and pink floral skirt and added strappy sandals. Standing sideways, she groaned, noticing the slight roundness to her stomach.

Who was she kidding? The man knew she'd had a baby ten days ago. She leaned closer to check her makeup. She usually didn't wear any, just a little for special occasions. "Is proposing marriage special enough?" she asked the mirror.

She glanced down at her shaking hands. Her entire body was shaking. "Oh, stop it. The worst the man can do is turn you down." More than likely he'd just laugh in her face. She groaned. "Oh, I can't do this." Her gaze raised to the ceiling. The most important person in her life was asleep upstairs and depending on her. That alone gave her courage.

A sound outside caused Joy to gasp and to head to the back door. Gravel scattered as the dusty black truck came to a stop, and Chance jumped out and hurried toward her. He had on faded jeans and a blue shirt that hugged those wide shoulders. His hat was cocked low over steel-gray eyes that always seemed to stare right through her. Her stomach tightened as he made it to the porch in one leap and suddenly stood in front of her.

"Is something wrong with the baby?" he asked.

"Oh…no, she's fine." She had trouble talking. More like trouble breathing. "She's asleep."

Chance came through the door she held open for him. "Then what's the emergency?"

Joy swallowed, reacting to his too-close presence. As he brushed by her, she inhaled a mixture of animals and the man himself. "There…really isn't one. I just needed to talk to you."

He removed his hat and wiped his damp forehead

with his sleeve. He looked as if he'd just come from the range. "Ella said to get over to the Kirby place fast."

She shook her head. "I told her whenever it was convenient for you. Sorry if I took you away from your work."

"We're getting ready for roundup," he said. "Things are hectic. But, now that I'm here, what do you need?"

Joy fought losing her nerve. "How badly do you want the ranch?"

His gaze narrowed as if he didn't trust what he'd just heard. "I think you know the answer to that. I'll offer you a fair price, even help you get settled in town—"

"No, I'm not moving out." She glanced away from his mesmerizing gaze. "But I want to offer you a deal."

Silently, he waited.

Joy ignored her drumming heart and rushed on, "If you want the ranch you'll have to marry me."

Outside of a quick blink of his eyes, Chance Randell seemed to continue to stand impassively.

She hurried on to explain, "I'm in a situation where I need a husband. If…if you marry me, I'm willing to sell you part of my land."

He just stood there. A quick no would suffice. His saying nothing was so humiliating.

"Could you at least give me the courtesy of saying something?"

"Lady, you caught me a little off guard." He looked at his hat as he played with the brim. "This isn't what I expected to hear."

"Believe me, I don't go around asking men I've only known a few days to marry me."

"Want to fill me in on the reason you decided to ask me?" he asked.

She drew a long breath and released it. "Since my husband's death seven months ago, my in-laws have been threatening to take my baby. They have a lot of money…and power. I left Denver because I was afraid of them. That's the reason this ranch means so much. I need a home for Katie and me. Right now they have no idea where I am, but it shouldn't take them long to find out." Joy walked to the coffeepot, poured two cups and carried them to the table.

Stunned, Chance's gaze feasted on his petite neighbor. Wearing a skirt that gave him a peek at her shapely legs she looked soft and pretty. The top she wore hugged her full breasts and slimmed her waist. Feeling his pulse quicken, he bit back a groan. Hell, Joy Spencer had been on his mind for three miserable days. She was all he could think of. So much so, his overnight trip to Midland hadn't included a visit with Nita.

Damn! Now, she had him racing out here, and the minute he walked though the door, she sucker-punched him.

Joy drew his attention back. "I know this is a surprise.…"

"I'd use a little stronger word. Like *shock*."

Suddenly she looked so fragile. "Chance, I have no choice."

He ought to tell her she had a lot more options than marrying a Randell.

"Besides what I'm offering you is a business deal.

I don't *want* a husband, I *need* one to help me keep Katie.''

That was the clincher. Katie Rose. He had helped bring the child into the world, and he would never let anything or anyone harm her.

''I'm offering to sell you two sections of land for every year we stay married. We can draw up a contract, spelling out everything legally.''

Chance could tell she was feeling as awkward about this as he was. He desperately wanted the ranch, but he didn't want it this way. ''Look, I'm not the best person for this. I wouldn't be good father material.''

Joy Spencer's tender gaze locked with his. ''That's not so, Chance. I've watched you with my daughter.'' She walked up to him. ''The only reason I'm asking you is because I know you care about Katie.''

Chance didn't want to care. He'd tried not to, but the baby had gotten to him. At least he knew where he stood with the child. What about the mother?

''Exactly what kind of husband are you expecting?''

Joy's face reddened immediately. She shook her head. ''Oh, no. I don't expect you to share my bed. I mean, I can't expect you...I loved only one man, and he's gone. This marriage will be for security.''

''A business agreement,'' he confirmed.

She nodded. ''But there is one thing. You'll need to move into the house. We have to look married, if only to convince the Spencers and a judge. Your private life can go on as usual.'' She gasped. ''Oh, gosh, I never thought about you having someone in your life. I mean if there's a woman...?''

He raised his hands. ''No, there isn't anyone. There hasn't been for a long time,'' he confessed. ''But there's something I should tell you." He paused, watching the brightness in her eyes, praying it wasn't going to change. "Around here the name *Randell* leaves a bad taste in some folks' mouths. My father wasn't exactly a model citizen...."

"I know Jack Randell was sent to prison for cattle rustling."

He couldn't help but blink. Had someone warned her against him? "So you investigated me."

"I asked one person, Aunt Lil's lawyer, John Gilbert. He had nothing but good things to say about you. I only did it because of Katie."

He nodded. "Did John also tell you that I wasn't exactly a model teenager?"

She nodded, fighting a smile. "I believe he said you and your brothers were 'hell on wheels' until Hank Barrett took you in and made you toe the line."

"I guess that pretty much says it." Excitement raced through him. She knew about his past, and she still wanted him. Whoa...what was he thinking? She wanted a man—a husband—not him. But she was dangling everything he'd ever wanted in front of him. Could he accept it?

He saw the expectant look on her face. "I'm going to need a day or so to think about this. So should you."

She released a long breath and nodded.

"How soon do you want this marriage to take place?"

"I think, as soon as possible. I mean, if my in-laws appear at my door, I need to show them I've made my child a good home."

Chance nodded and stood in front of her, breathing in her sweet fragrance. "I have one request, Joy. If we decide to go through with this marriage, I don't want anyone to know about our arrangement. As far as everyone else is concerned, we would truly be husband and wife.''

The next day, Chance was in the barn checking on his mare's new foal. It was too early to tell, but as far as he was concerned, the two-day-old colt, Stormy Night, was perfect. The roan had four neat white stockings covering long spindly legs. But Chance could tell by the colt's size and build he was a prize quarter horse. Everything he'd hoped for and more. In a few years, with the horse's impressive bloodline, he expected he'd bring top dollar in stud fees.

''He's a beauty, isn't he?''

Chance looked away from the stall to find Hank beside him. ''I keep looking for a flaw but can't find a one,'' Chance said.

Hank grinned. ''So you've decided to keep this guy?''

Chance nodded. ''You were right to breed Sweetness with Lightning. I wasn't sure the stud fee was worth it.''

The older man took off his hat. ''Can't say I was totally sure myself, but something told me those two would be a good mix. Besides, this guy's daddy was a champion cutting horse. At the very least you'll get a good cow horse.''

''I count on your instincts.'' Chance hadn't realized how much he depended on Hank's judgment. They strolled down the concrete aisle in the horse barn, passing several enclosed stalls, half of them filled with mares in season. Chance stopped and rubbed the nose of the chestnut that he'd brought back from Midland.

Soon, he hoped, every stall would be filled, and he could even expand the operation to the Kirby Ranch. It had a good-sized barn where he could keep horses. He'd just need to build some new stalls.

Okay fella, slow down, he told himself. He hadn't decided if he was going to accept Joy's offer.

They strolled outside into the sunlight, and Hank turned to him. "Have you scheduled the roundup?"

Chance nodded. "I've hired eight hands, the ones who worked last year. Most of the neighbors are willing to help out too. So, a week from Wednesday, if everything goes all right, we can start, and we should be finished by Saturday evening." And maybe he and Joy could be married this weekend. He blinked at the thought, realizing he was seriously considering her proposal. He'd weighed the pros and cons of her idea all night. It made sense for them to join forces. He wanted her land, and she needed a father for Katie. What more was there to think about?

"Hank, there's something I need to talk to you about."

"Sure, son, what is it?"

Together they headed along the tree-lined path toward the house. "I wanted to let you know, I'm thinking about getting married this weekend."

Hank paused as if to say something, then continued to the large porch and sat down in the chair he used most evenings, weather permitting. "Are you going to let me know who the lucky gal is, or do I have to guess?"

Chance leaned against one of the white pillars. "It's Joy Spencer."

Hank studied him for a while. "Son, you're old enough to know what you're doing, but don't you

think you two should get to know one other a little
better?"

"Our marriage is going to be a little different than
most. She needs a father for her baby." Chance
shrugged. "I told her that I didn't fit the bill in that
department, but she insisted I did." The two men
gazed at each other for a minute. Chance couldn't lie
to Hank. "Her in-laws may try to take away her
daughter. She feels if she's married, chances of that
happening would be less."

"I have a feeling there's more to this than that."

"In a year, if we stay married, she'll sell me two
sections of land."

Hank leaned back in his chair with a sigh. Chance
knew he wouldn't have to wait long to know what the
man was thinking. "You know, love might be a better
way to go," Hank finally said.

Chance pulled off his hat. Although he'd never met
Hank's wife, he knew the two had had a loving marriage. "Not all of us are cut out for love."

The older man nodded. "I see. Well, I guess people
have gotten married for a lot less."

Early the next morning, Joy fed Katie, then brought
her downstairs to the kitchen and placed her carrier on
the table. "So are you going to keep me company
while I have my breakfast?"

Katie cooed, then decided that her fist would taste
good. Joy smiled and went to start the coffeepot. There
was a knock at the back door.

Oh, no—Chance. She tightened her robe and
smoothed her hair. Well, he deserved to see what he
would get at this hour of the morning, she thought.

She went though the mudroom—ignoring the whining puppies—to the door. She was surprised to find an older man with a full head of thick white hair. He had on jeans and a neatly pressed white shirt covered with a brown leather vest. His hat was in his hand, along with a brown sack.

"Hello, Mrs. Spencer. I'm Hank Barrett from the Circle B."

Joy smiled. "Mr. Barrett, it's so nice to meet you."

He glanced at her attire and frowned. "I'm sorry, I see I've come too early."

She opened the screen door. "No, it's all right. I've been up for hours. I just haven't had a chance to dress. Please, come in."

He stepped into the mudroom. "I see you got some of the Campbells' pups."

"Yes, Ella thought I needed a watchdog, and I ended up with two."

They went into the kitchen. Hank looked around the room. "Gosh, I haven't been in here in probably ten years. Hasn't changed much."

"I don't think my aunt redid anything. It needs work."

"If everything is in working order it's fine. I think you have enough to do without worrying about re-modeling the house."

Joy nodded. "May I offer you some coffee?"

"If it's not too much trouble. It would go good with the cinnamon rolls I brought."

"Oh, did Ella bake those?"

Hank's laughter filled the room. "No, I stopped by a bakery in town. It's safer that way."

Joy had no idea what he was talking about. She brought a cup over to the table, but the rancher was more interested in seeing the baby.

"I take it this is Katie Rose."

"Yes, this is my daughter."

"I hear you caused quite a ruckus a few weeks ago." Hank touched the baby's cheek, and she grabbed his finger. "Well, would you look at that. You've got quite a grip there."

"It's unbelievable how strong she is," Joy said.

His kind hazel eyes met hers. "I'm sorry it's taken me so long to come by and welcome you."

"It's okay. We've had a lot of company. Ella and several women from the local church have been looking in on me and Katie. Everyone has been so friendly and helpful."

"Between Ella and Chance, I feel as if I already know you." Katie released Hank's finger. "Chance talks about you all the time."

Her breath caught. "He does?"

"Well, of course," Hank said as he nodded toward the baby. "He did help bring this little filly into the world. I think she's stolen his heart. And I can see why. She's going to be a real heartbreaker."

"Look, Mr. Barrett—"

"It's Hank," he corrected.

"Hank, would you like to stay for breakfast? I was just going to cook some eggs, and we can add the rolls you brought." She glanced down at her attire. "If you wouldn't mind keeping an eye on Katie for a few minutes, I'll put on some clothes."

A big grin split his weathered face. "Wouldn't mind at all, ma'am."

Joy hurried upstairs and tore off her robe and gown. She grabbed a pair of jeans from the drawer along with a T-shirt that read Denver Broncos. She slipped on her tennis shoes, went into the bathroom and groaned at the sight of her wild mane. She definitely was going to get a haircut…soon. She didn't have time to mess with styling her hair. After working a brush through the long strands, she managed to do a French braid. She brushed her teeth and applied a little lipstick, then hurried downstairs to find another visitor in her kitchen.

Hank was still fussing over the baby while Chance leaned against the kitchen counter drinking coffee.

She sucked in a breath as she took in his long lean body covered in worn jeans and western shirt. A warm tingle went through her as her gaze moved to his forearms, then to the large hands that cradled the coffee mug. She knew from experience that those work-hardened hands could be gentle, too.

"Morning, Joy." His voice was husky and deep as he reached for a cup and offered it to her.

She walked over and accepted the mug. "Thank you."

His gray eyes roamed over her attire and she could feel her body heat up as he eyed her T-shirt. "You better get rid of that shirt if you want to survive around here. You're in Cowboys country."

So the man had a sense of humor. "I'll think about it." She turned and went to Hank.

"How was she?"

"She was an angel."

"Okay, since she's being good, I'll start on that breakfast I promised. How about bacon and eggs? Unless you've already eaten."

The old rancher grinned. "It's been hours."

"Okay." She smiled and looked at Chance. "How about you? You hungry, too?"

"You don't have to go to so much trouble," Chance said.

"It's no trouble," she assured him. "I was going to eat anyway." She went to the refrigerator and took out the ingredients she needed.

Chance came over beside her. "I'll help."

"No need. I enjoy cooking." She glanced into his steel-gray eyes, uneasy with his closeness. "You could set the table," she suggested.

He nodded, went to the cupboard, took down three plates and arranged them at the table while Hank continued to play with Katie.

His task finished, he returned to her side again. "Looks like Katie got a new playmate," he said quietly, nodding at Hank.

"Isn't it sweet?" Joy was touched. If she and Chance married, Hank would be like a grandfather to her daughter. How would he feel about that?

"I've never seen that man turned into mush before."

Joy smiled. "Babies can do that to a person."

He leaned closer, and she could smell the clean scent of his soap. He whispered near her cheek, "If you haven't changed your mind, I accept your offer."

Joy stopped in the middle of breaking an egg into the bowl. "What?" She swallowed, hoping she heard him right. He was going to marry her?

"Have you changed your mind?" His voice was low, ensuring that Hank couldn't hear their discussion.

"No...no, I haven't changed my mind."

He nodded. "Okay, but there's one other thing."

Joy held her breath. He wanted more. "I thought I offered you a fair deal."

He shook his head. "You did. This is concerning Katie."

"Katie?"

"Yes. I want you to know that I'll do everything I can to protect her. If you need anything made legal. I mean…if it helps with the custody."

Joy couldn't believe this man. One minute he wanted her gone, the next he was offering a safe haven for her and her child. She met his silver gaze and a strange sensation erupted in her stomach. She glanced away. "That's very kind of you."

He shrugged. "No kid should have to go through an adult war."

She smiled sadly, wondering if he and his brothers had. "No, they shouldn't. But let's not worry about that right now. You marrying me should be enough for now."

"Okay, then let's do it. We can be married this weekend."

"So soon?"

"I have roundup starting the middle of next week."

"Oh, then I guess it's this weekend."

Joy stood in the bride's room of the River Walk Chapel and brushed the imaginary wrinkles from her dress, a soft pale-pink sheath that flattered her still-rounded body.

After hearing the news of the upcoming wedding, Ella had insisted they go shopping for the special day. Joy hadn't put up a fight, especially when she'd discovered she couldn't fit into most of her own clothes yet. She needed to work out after the doctor gave her the go-ahead to start exercising.

Right now she had to concentrate on what she was

about to do. Panic raced through her, and she began to pace. She was about to marry a virtual stranger. No, Chance Randell wasn't exactly that. He was a good man. He'd helped bring Katie into the world. He'd been kind to both of them.

Ella walked into the room carrying Katie in her arms. "You look beautiful."

"Thank you. I just wish I wasn't so nervous." The older woman had been wonderful to her, and never once had she questioned the rushed marriage.

"Every bride feels this way," the housekeeper said. "Chance is a lucky guy to get you and this little one."

"Thank you for saying that. I'm pretty lucky, too."

The older woman sobered. "You are, Joy. There's no finer man than Chance. He needs a good woman more than he knows."

Joy wanted to scream she wasn't the woman who could give Chance what he needed...her heart.

"Come on, there's an anxious groom waiting." Ella opened the door, and they went to the back of the chapel where they were met by the wedding coordinator. She handed Joy a bouquet of spring flowers. "Your soon-to-be husband said to give you these."

"Chance got me flowers?" Joy was surprised by his thoughtfulness. But why not? He'd suggested the chapel instead of just going to city hall.

The music began and Ella and Katie started down the short aisle. Then it was Joy's turn. On shaky legs, she made her way down the carpet. She looked up and, for the first time, saw the handsome man waiting for her.

Chance was dressed in a black western-cut suit, and a snowy white shirt showed off his tanned skin. His sandy hair was cut and combed off his forehead, but strands were threatening to fall. Their eyes met as she stopped in front of him. She looked for some sort of panic, but surprisingly he winked at her.

Chance took her hand in his and they turned toward the minister. Joy tried to concentrate on the words he spoke, but it seemed impossible. Somehow she managed to recite her vows, and before she knew it, he had pronounced them man and wife.

"You may kiss your bride," he said.

Chance turned to Joy. Her heart began to drum in her chest as his eyes locked with hers. Then as if in slow motion, Chance reached for her and drew her close. He bent his head as Joy's pulse raced in her ears, but she found herself raising her chin to meet his kiss. Her lashes drifted shut just as his lips touched hers. Then a warm rush went through her and a stirring began low in her stomach as his mouth moved over hers. Finally he released her, but his silver gaze held hers, revealing he'd been just as affected by the kiss as she.

Hank slapped Chance on the back. "Congratulations." Then he leaned over and kissed Joy on the cheek. "Welcome to the family. Now let's go celebrate. It's not every day a person gets married."

"No, not every day," Chance repeated still looking at her.

A warm shiver went through Joy as she kept telling herself she had done the right thing.

But no matter right or wrong, she'd just married a virtual stranger.

Chapter Six

By seven that evening, Chance pulled into the drive and parked his truck by the back door of the Kirby Ranch. He turned to Joy. "We're here."

She didn't meet his gaze. "I guess we are."

The tension was so thick between them he could barely breathe. "I'm sorry about Ella putting you in an awkward position about staying the night in town. She was only trying to make the day special."

"I know," she said. "I guess we're going to have to be prepared for more situations like this."

"Would you rather have stayed at the inn?"

She shook her head. "No. I mean, I have the baby."

Chance glanced into the back seat at the sleeping baby. "Katie was a good excuse to turn down the offer, though."

At the mention of her name, the infant stirred and began to fuss. "And now she's also hungry," Joy said.

"Right." Chance jumped down from the truck and hurried around to the passenger side. He opened Joy's door and helped her out, then reached in and unfastened Katie's carrier. With his precious burden in one arm, he assisted his new wife to the porch and let her unlock the door. Once inside, he handed over her baby.

"You go on and feed her," he said. "I'll bring in my things. What bedroom should I use?"

He watched her blush. "I...I prepared the room at the end of the hall. Beside my room. It's the largest."

She avoided his gaze, and it bothered him. "Look, Joy, it's okay. I can sleep anywhere as long as I have a bed...." But one look at her told him where he wanted to sleep. Her room. "I'll be fine."

Katie began crying in earnest, which started the puppies whimpering. "I better get her fed."

"Right, and I'll unload the truck." He backed out the door, wondering what had gotten into him. He shouldn't be thinking about Joy in any way but as a business partner. Getting involved with her would only cause him trouble. But that didn't mean he hadn't thought she looked beautiful today. When she'd walked down the aisle at the chapel, she had taken his breath away. For a second or two he couldn't help but fantasize that she was really his bride. *His.*

"Forget it, Randell. She's off limits. She's meant to be with a man who doesn't come with a past. A man who can give her everything...including love. You aren't cut out to do that." He walked to the bed of his truck and lifted out his suitcases. After the ceremony and lunch this afternoon, they'd stopped by the Circle B to pick up some of his things, while Ella gave Joy a quick tour of the ranch house. Luckily, Katie'd begun to fuss, or they'd still be there with Ella telling boring stories about him as a kid.

Chance carried his suitcases up the porch. He had bigger problems now. Like how he was going to find a way to live like a monk in the same house with a beautiful woman.

Joy sat in the rocker holding Katie to her breast, humming softly as her daughter suckled hungrily. One of the best things about Katie Rose was her great appetite.

A creaking on the stairs distracted Joy as she listened for Chance. He passed her bedroom and continued down the hall, then finally she heard the clink of his door closing. He was moving in.

She let out a breath. Had she made a mistake today? Had she acted too hastily with this marriage? The Spencers hadn't even found her yet. She glanced down at Katie, brushed her fingers over her down-covered head, and remembered just days ago when Chance Randell had promised to protect her. Something inside Joy told her that he would.

She lifted her daughter to her shoulder and began patting her back. After Katie burped, Joy settled her baby at her other breast. A soft knock on the bedroom door startled her. She reached for a blanket and covered herself.

"Yes, come in."

The door opened and Chance stepped just inside. He had removed his jacket, and his sleeves were rolled up to expose his muscular forearms.

"I was wondering how long you were going to be." His eyes never wavered from her face. "I was going to fix some supper."

"Oh, you don't need to cook."

"I was only going to grill some steaks, bake a couple potatoes and make a salad. Are you hungry?"

She nodded. She'd been too nervous to eat earlier today. "I could eat something. If you give me a few minutes I'll help you."

"You can make the salad." He started to leave and stopped. "You looked pretty today, Joy…in your dress."

"Thank you," she said. She had changed into her robe before she began feeding Katie. "You looked nice today, too."

"Not every day a man gets married." He turned and walked out.

Joy blinked. She and Chance were actually married. In the eyes of the law at least, they were husband and wife.

Fifteen minutes later, Katie finished her feeding and fell asleep before her mother even put her in her crib. Joy slipped her dress back on and checked her makeup, telling herself that it was just as easy as finding something else to wear tonight.

She went down to the kitchen and found that two places had been set at the long oak table in the dining room, with the nice china and stemware from her aunt's hutch. So, Chance had planned their wedding supper.

In the kitchen, she found Chance bending over to check the steaks sizzling in the broiler. His black suit pants were pulled tight over his firm butt and muscular legs. Oh, my, she might have just had a baby, but there certainly wasn't anything wrong with her hormones!

As if Chance sensed her presence, he stood and turned around. His gaze moved over her and he smiled. "You're in time to make the salad, I just turned the steaks." He pointed to the ingredients on the counter.

She walked across the room and eyed the tomatoes, lettuce and cucumbers. "Where did you get all this stuff?"

"Ella's garden. When I took a couple of steaks from the freezer, she handed me a large bag of vegetables. She may not be the best cook in the world, but she can grow anything."

"I'll have to thank her," she said as she rinsed the lettuce. "I've eaten pretty much everything the ladies brought over, and I haven't had a chance to get to the store." She felt terrible. Her new husband had to bring his own food.

"If you make a list, I can pick up whatever you need in town tomorrow."

She tore the lettuce and dropped the pieces into the bowl. "Put diapers on top."

"Done. You need them tonight?" He came up next to her and picked up the cucumber and washed it off, then began slicing it. A warmth spread through her as she watched his large, capable hands at work.

He glanced at her, and she realized she hadn't answered him. "No, tomorrow is soon enough."

"If you like, you and Katie could go with me, that way you won't forget anything." He raised an eyebrow. "Unless you don't want to go out so soon. I mean, I know it's only been a few weeks since you gave birth."

"No, I'm fine. Really. I don't think I'm ready to run a marathon, but I feel good. I could tackle the grocery store. But don't you have work to do…at the Circle B?"

"This is supposed to be my honeymoon," he said. "The guys at the ranch would never let me live it down if I showed up for work tomorrow morning. I'll get harassed enough when we start the roundup in a few days." He pulled open the oven door and stabbed a fork into the potatoes, checking their readiness, then took them out, along with two huge steaks. "Looks like it's time to eat." He carried the platter into the dining room.

Joy finished up the salad and followed after him. She placed the glass bowl on the table as Chance walked around and pulled out her chair.

"Thank you." She sat down, suddenly feeling the shared intimacy.

He went back to the kitchen, then returned with butter, salad dressing and a bottle of sparkling cider. "Ella slipped this into the bag, too. She says a toast on our wedding day is good luck." He frowned. "But if you'd rather not...?"

"Oh, no, I would like to." Her voice drifted into a hushed whisper.

He opened the bottle and poured them each a glass.

He looked at her, his eyes silver. She couldn't seem to look away.

"What should we toast?" she asked.

He sat down in the chair opposite her. "To a good life for all three of us."

Their glasses touched, sending a chiming sound into the silent air as Joy prayed that Chance's words would come true.

Joy heard crying in the distance. Katie. Her eyes shot open as her head jerked up from the pillow. She brushed her hair from her face and stumbled out of bed.

"I'm coming, Katie," she called, realizing sunlight was streaming through the window blind.

She rushed through the double doors that connected her room to the small nursery, only to discover Chance standing beside the crib. He was dressed in a pair of jeans and nothing else. Against his gloriously naked chest he was cradling a crying Katie. Where had he come from? She glanced at the opened door leading in from the hallway.

He turned to her. "I thought I could quiet her so you could sleep awhile longer."

Joy fidgeted with a wayward lock of hair and pushed it behind her ear. She looked down at her plain cotton gown that didn't hide much. Next time she had to remember her robe. "Nothing quiets her when she's hungry."

Just then the baby made a loud sucking noise. "I guess I'm not equipped to feed her," he said, carefully handing Joy the baby. In the exchange his hand brushed her breast.

If Chance noticed the contact, he didn't show it. "I'll go start the coffee." He left the room, leaving Joy tingling—and not from the rush of her milk.

Chance hurried into his bedroom and grabbed a T-shirt and a pair of socks. Damn, he wouldn't do that again. He should have known better than to go into the nursery. Of course, with them all living together, he was bound to run into Joy often. What caught him off guard was he hadn't expected to see her in a flimsy nightgown that left nothing to the imagination. The memory sent hot blood coursing through his veins as he went down the stairs and into the kitchen.

With the coffee started, he went to the porch and greeted the puppies. "Come on, girls, let's go outside a while. I need a shot of cool air." He lifted them from the box, and carried them out to the high grass, letting them wander around. The morning sun was just starting to warm the spring air.

Grabbing his boots, he sat on the bottom step and pulled on his socks, trying to block out what had happened just moments ago. Hell, how could he? He leaned back, releasing a long sigh. How could he forget Joy looking all soft and warm from sleep? At least she'd gotten some. He'd spent the night trying to find a way to stop seeing her face every time he closed his eyes.

When he felt something tugging at his sock, he looked down to find that little Sunny had taken an interest in his big toe. He smiled at the puppy's playfulness, and she soon wandered off.

Chance knew he had to find something to do to keep his mind off Joy, especially the next two days when he had to stay so close to the house, pretending they were honeymooners. His gaze roamed around the neglected yard, the weed-infested flower bed and faded porch furniture. One thing he'd remembered about Lillian Kirby, she kept this ranch in top shape. "I bet you're not happy about the way the place looks, Miss Kirby."

Chance remembered the riding mower in the barn. At least he would stay busy today. He scooped up the dogs and went inside. He'd worry about tomorrow later. His new motto was one day at a time.

Joy heard the commotion when she came downstairs. She set Katie's carrier on the table and poured herself some coffee. Carrying her mug, she went to the back porch and found Chance on a mower, working hard at cutting the grass.

Well, it did need it, she thought. She went back into the kitchen and decided she'd better come up with some breakfast for her hungry husband. Husband. Suddenly she felt strangely disloyal to Blake. No, this wasn't a real marriage. There would never be another man she loved as she had loved her husband—Katie's father. But she needed Chance, and he needed her.

She pulled milk and four eggs from the refrigerator and began whipping up a batch of pancakes. By the time she took the last of a tall stack off the grill, the mower had stopped. A few moments after that, Chance walked inside. He took off his hat and hung it on the hook.

"Good morning," he said. His white T-shirt was dirty from his labor. So were his hands and arms.

"Good morning. Looks like you've been busy."

"We start early here in Texas to get ahead of the heat."

"Well, I hope you can take time for breakfast. You like pancakes?"

"I've been known to eat my share." He went to the sink and turned on the water.

"Then you can get started on these."

"Thanks."

"Where did the mower come from?"

"The barn," he said as he lathered up. "Just took me a while to get it started."

"Well, thanks for cutting the grass. I didn't know what I was going to do about it."

He dried his hands, walked to the table, peeked at

Katie and sat down. "Well, you don't have to worry anymore. I can handle the grass."

She returned to the table with two mugs of coffee. "I didn't mean for you to have to do any work."

He buttered his stack, then poured a generous amount of syrup. "What exactly did you think I was going to do? Sit all day?"

"No, I mean," she began. What did she expect him to do? "I thought you were going to be working at the Circle B."

"I will, but I'll also be taking care of things around here that have been neglected for the past few years. I'm going to be living here, too."

She sighed. "I know, Chance, but I feel I should be handling things."

"You will, but right now, you have a baby to care for and your doctor wouldn't be happy with me if I let you overdo it."

"Surely there's something I can help you with."

A smile appeared on his face, and a fluttering erupted in her stomach. "I like you cooking my breakfast."

"That I can do."

He took a bite of her pancakes and groaned. "These are wonderful."

"Thanks, I love to cook. I just haven't done much lately, not since…" Her voice drifted off as thoughts of Blake came rushing back.

"You can talk about your husband, Joy."

"I know. It's just that…I feel funny. I always thought I'd be married to Blake forever and now…everything has changed." She looked at the new gold band on her finger.

As if her words hadn't registered at all, Chance continued to eat, then he finally spoke, "Nothing's changed," he said. "Nothing that matters anyway."

He took another large bite of his pancakes, and she went back to the stove and poured some more batter on the hot grill. One big difference between the two men was Chance's appetite—it was much larger than Blake's had been.

"After I finish the yard work," he said, "I want to run some ideas by you."

"I told you you can do anything you want with the land." Joy came back to the table with four more pancakes.

He dumped the stack on his plate. "I'd never do anything without checking with you, but we need to discuss your plans for the pecan orchard. In the past your aunt had a company come out and harvest the crop. You still have another six months to decide what to do." He poured more syrup on the cakes. "And you talked about a vegetable garden. I could till the soil and get some starter plants. Ella could probably help you, too."

Chance's enthusiasm was contagious. "I'd like that."

"Can you wait until next week? I'm going to be pretty busy with the roundup." He eyed her. "So will you. Now that I know you can cook, you can help feed the crew."

She smiled, liking the thought of being part of the family. "Whatever you want me to do."

He paused from his eating and grinned. "Think you can teach Ella how to cook?"

Later that afternoon, they drove into town. "What's your specialty?" Chance asked as he pushed the cart down the aisle.

Joy headed to the baby section. "My specialty?"

"All good cooks have a favorite dish they like to make."

"Well, that all depends..." Joy paused at the diaper display. She found her brand and placed several bags in the cart. "I do lasagna, beef Stroganoff, beef roasts and chicken dishes. Several different kinds of casseroles."

"How about fried chicken?" Chance asked.

No challenge, she thought. "I can fry chicken."

"Potato salad and beans?"

She nodded. "I can make those."

"Good. That will be perfect for the roundup."

"You sure that's all you want? I mean, back in Denver, my friend, Terri, and I used to do some catering. I could make something a little more exciting than fried chicken."

"Thanks for the offer, but ranch hands like simple food." Chance smiled. "Of course, *I* wouldn't mind sampling anything else you have in mind."

Joy's heart raced at his words, trying to tell herself he only meant food. Then she caught the glint in his silver eyes and began to wonder. Keep it light, she told herself. "You better be careful, Chance Randell. Not all my dishes turn out to be winners."

"I doubt that, Mrs. Randell. I can handle it. Remember I've been raised on Ella's cooking."

She blinked in surprise as he called her by her new name. Before she could say anything, a woman came toward them—an attractive brunette with a small child sitting in her cart.

"Well, would you looky here, Chance Randell in the baby section."

Chance stiffened. "Hello, Cindy."

"Hello, Chance. Haven't seen you around in a while."

"Been busy with the ranch."

The woman eyed Joy closely, then glanced down at Katie asleep in the cart. "With more than cattle and horses, I see."

The last person Chance needed to run into was Cindy Freeman. Besides being one of the town's biggest gossips, she was his old girlfriend Belinda's cousin. "Cindy Freeman, this is my...my wife, Joy Randell."

Shock was evident on the woman's face, then she recovered. "It's nice to meet you, Joy." She tossed a quick glance at Chance, then turned back to Joy. "How did you manage to catch one of the wild Randells?"

Joy looked up at Chance and gave him a dazzling smile as her arm slipped around his waist. "I guess I just got lucky." His heart pounded, wondering how far she was going to carry this. Then she stood up on tiptoes and pressed a kiss against his cheek. When she pulled back, her blue eyes met his. "Chance, don't you think we should be getting home?"

"Sure," he said, forcing himself to remember this all was just pretend. "Nice seeing you again, Cindy."

Cindy nodded. "It was. I'll tell Belinda you said hi."

Chance wanted to deny ever knowing Belinda, but he couldn't. He knew it gave Cindy a charge to remind him of his roots. He grabbed Joy by the arm and together they moved down the aisle.

They finished their shopping in twenty minutes, and

made it home and into the kitchen before Joy questioned him.

"You want to tell me who she is?" she asked. "I mean, did I take you away from someone?"

"No." He wanted to make an excuse to go outside, but he figured he owed her an explanation. "Belinda is just a woman I dated a while back."

She continued to watch him.

"About five years ago, Belinda came to visit San Angelo for the summer. They came out to the Circle B looking to buy one of my saddle horses, and Belinda showed an interest in me. Of course, I ate it up." He raked a hand through his hair. "Hell, I knew I was out of my league, but it didn't stop me. To her, it was just a bet with Cindy that she could…be with one of the wild Randells. She was slumming. Anyway, it was over quickly. By August Belinda went back to Dallas. End of story."

"Oh, Chance, I'm sorry."

"Look, I don't need your pity." He started to walk out, but Joy put her hand on his arm.

"I didn't think I was offering any," she said. "Just compassion. The same as you've given me because I lost my husband. Belinda shouldn't have treated you that way. No one has a right to use people."

Chance could see the fierceness in her eyes. It touched him. "It was a long time ago." He shrugged. "I never think about her." *Not since you and Katie came into my life, anyway.* Where did that come from? He shouldn't forget the pain Belinda caused, reminding him he wasn't cut out for love.

"Still it wasn't right." Joy clenched her fist. "I better not run into Cindy again, or I might just give her a piece of my mind."

Chance took her fist in his hand. "You don't need to stand up for me, Joy. I'm a Randell, I've become pretty immune to this."

"Oh, Chance." She raised her hand to his cheek. He felt like he'd been scorched. "No one is immune when it comes to their heart."

He had to get away from her. He covered her hand with his and slowly moved it away. "I think we should get these groceries put away before Katie wakes up."

Joy nodded, then glanced away as if she'd been just as affected by their closeness as he was. "Yeah, she's been so good all day."

They began emptying the sacks and filling cupboards. Once the task was done, Joy announced she was preparing lasagna for dinner.

Chance had to get away. They'd gotten too close, and he couldn't let that happen. "I have some things to do out in the barn. But if you need me to stay, I will."

"No, I can handle things here. I'll feed Katie and put her down, then start on dinner."

He nodded, grabbed his hat off the hook and walked out the door, only stopping to release the puppies and take them along. He marched across the freshly mowed lawn with an excited Ginger and Sunny close on his heels. Then he went into the barn, continuing past the empty stalls, trying to focus on the new construction he had planned for his horses. But all that filled his mind was what he couldn't have. The one thing he could never have.

Drawn to the tack room where it had all begun, he glanced around. The floor was covered with straw. A row of dust-covered harnesses hung from hooks on the walls. A single window filtered light throughout the room to the bare cot where Joy had given birth to Katie.

Had it been only weeks ago when he'd helped bring the tiny baby into the world? He sat down on the canvas bed and remembered how Joy had clung to him, how she had trusted him when he'd asked her for one more push. Then the glorious look in her bright, tear-filled eyes when he'd handed her the baby. Now she'd asked him for help again.

He picked up the chocolate puppy and stroked her as the other continued to wander around. It would be easy to accept how perfect this situation was. How on the outside, his marriage seemed so real. But he didn't get to touch her, sleep with her, make love with her. Somehow he had to remember it was only pretend. Joy didn't love him...and he would never truly be her husband.

The cold reality of the fact hit him hard. And it hurt.

Chapter Seven

Joy's excitement grew Tuesday afternoon as Chance drove his truck under the Circle B's archway. Another hundred yards along the gravel road took them by several pristine whitewashed outbuildings.

She eyed the row of trucks and horse trailers parked alongside a large barn. A group of cowboys were talking under the shade of an old oak tree. They were all here for the roundup tomorrow. Chance continued toward the corral where a dozen or so horses roamed freely, the magnificent animals' coats glistening in the warm Texas sun.

"Oh, they're beautiful, Chance," she said, unable to take her eyes off the spectacular sight. "Are they all yours?"

"Most of them. You like horses?"

"Oh, yes, but I was raised in the city. I've only gone riding once in my life." Living on the ranch, she'd hoped to have one of her own.

"I could teach you."

Joy couldn't contain her enthusiasm. "You mean it? Really? Oh, Chance that would be wonderful."

He raised a hand. "I can't this minute, but maybe in a few weeks after I bring some of the horses over to the ranch. And when your doctor says you can ride."

She didn't want to wait. "But I feel fine now."

"That's good, but you just had a baby a month ago. So we're going to take it slow. How about later I take you down to the barn and introduce you to our newest colt?"

She turned to Chance and smiled. "I'd like that."

"Okay, after I get you and Katie settled."

Chance pulled the truck up next to the two-story gray house with the white shutters. He climbed out and went around the truck as he waved to the men. He opened Joy's door and helped her down, then he released Katie's carrier and lifted her out. He took Joy's arm and they walked toward the back of the house.

"I'll need to go over to the bunkhouse and check on the men. But if you need me to hang around...?"

She shook her head. "I'm going to help Ella."

"Yeah, help her a lot." He smiled. "You're making fried chicken for tomorrow, right? I promised the guys you'd be cooking."

Joy gasped. "You're so bad, Chance Randell. I'm not going to hurt Ella's feelings and take over her kitchen."

"No, it's okay. I've already told her that you wanted to help with the food for the roundup. I said you have a special recipe for chicken. She's more than happy to share her kitchen with you."

Joy still wasn't convinced. "But what if she wants to make something?"

"She is. Baked beans."

"Is that *her* specialty?"

His smile broadened into a grin. "Oh, darlin', beans are about the only thing that Ella can't hurt."

"What an awful thing to say." They were both laughing by the time they approached the porch steps.

"I'm only speaking the truth," Chance said. "Just ask Ella. She'll admit she's not the best cook in the world, but she makes up for it in many other ways."

Joy didn't miss the tenderness that shone in his eyes as he spoke of the woman who'd helped raise him.

"She's a special woman."

"Yeah, Ella's special all right."

Chance escorted Joy inside the back door, through a large enclosed porch, then walked into the bright yellow kitchen. The room was a cook's delight with all the modern appliances and spacious tiled work areas one could want.

Suddenly Ella hurried in from the other room to greet them. "You're here." Dressed in her standard plaid shirt and jeans, she gave them both hugs, then looked down at Katie. "Hi, sweetie." As if Katie recognized her voice, she waved her arms. "Can I hold her?" Ella asked.

"Of course." Joy unstrapped her daughter and allowed the older woman to pick her up. While the housekeeper fussed over the baby, Chance carried in boxes holding a half-dozen pies and put them on the table.

"If you ladies don't need me, I'll head down to the barn and see if I can organize a roundup." He reached inside the box, broke off a piece of pie crust and popped it into his mouth.

"Hey, those are for tomorrow," Joy protested.

He grinned, and her pulse sped up. "Just sampling. Gotta see how good they are."

"You said that this morning," she argued. This was a lighthearted side of Chance that was foreign to her.

"It's my job," he insisted. "Wouldn't want you to bring pies that didn't taste just right." Smiling, he leaned closer to her. "They're all very good," he whispered. He lowered his head and placed a quick kiss on her lips. Even before she could catch her breath, he turned and headed for the door.

"Looks like you both got a little sugar to tide you over for a while," Ella said.

Joy wasn't paying attention. Her eyes were on the handsome cowboy who'd left her lips tingling for more. Darn him anyway, he wasn't supposed to kiss her. Then she realized he was only doing it for show. With a twinge of disappointment, Joy finally turned to Ella. "Well, we better get started on tomorrow's menu."

The housekeeper gave her a knowing smile. "I think we have plenty of time. So tell me, how are the newlyweds?"

"We're fine." Joy glanced away, then changed the subject. "How about I fix supper?" Joy said. "You can have the night off, and I'll make my special pot roast."

"I'd like that, but only if you let me take care of Katie." The gray-haired woman glanced at the baby in her arms, then at Joy. "And tell me if it's only your cooking that put that big grin on your cowboy's face."

"Well…" Just then her daughter began to cry. "I

better feed her before I start." Joy eagerly took the baby from Ella and glanced around the room. "Where can I go?" she asked.

"You'll have privacy upstairs. I've put you in Chance's old bedroom."

Ella led her through the doorway to the large dining room. They continued into the living room with its open-beam ceiling and windows that took up the entire wall, exposing a brick patio bordered with bright-hued flowers and a glorious view of the open pasture and hills beyond. Along another wall was a huge stone fireplace. A cream-colored rug partially covered the glossy hardwood floors. A brown leather sofa and two oversized chairs faced a large-screen television built into an oak cabinet. Joy followed Ella to the staircase and the second floor. They walked along an open railing that allowed a view of the great room below.

"I borrowed Libby Castle's granddaughter's crib. I hope Katie won't have any trouble sleeping."

At the second door, Ella escorted her inside to the big bedroom. Even though Chance had assured Joy he'd be sleeping in the bunkhouse during the roundup, she felt strange staying in his room. It seemed so...intimate. Too intimate for their arranged relationship.

Against one wall was a king-size bed covered by an Indian blanket in blues and browns. The pictures on the white walls were also Indian prints. The floor was carpeted in earth-tones. There was an alcove and a row of windows where an old rocker sat along with the crib.

"If you don't like it here..." Ella began.

"Oh, no, it's lovely."

"It's a man's room," the housekeeper said. "And

before that a boy's room. Since Chance came here, this was where he slept. His brothers' rooms are down the hall. They've been empty a long time now.'' There was a faraway look in Ella's eyes. Almost like a mother missing her child. She might not have been the Randell boys' biological mother, but she had been the closest they'd ever had.

"How long have Cade and Travis been gone?"

"Too long," Ella admitted. "Cade nearly ten years, Travis close to eight. Wouldn't be so bad, but they don't get home much. I know Hank doesn't say much, but he misses them a lot."

Katie began fussing again.

"Oh, goodness, listen to me go on," Ella said. "You feed that darling baby, and I'll bring up the diaper bag, then later one of the hands will bring your things up from the truck."

Once Ella left, Joy walked to the windows and looked down at the corral. She undid her blouse and bra and settled her daughter at her breast. When Katie was contentedly sucking, Joy's attention went to the corral where she saw Chance climb on one of the saddle horses. He took hold of the reins and rode the animal along the fence, putting him through several quick turns, then had him dance side to side. Joy found she was totally engrossed in the man. He rode like a natural. It was as if he and the animal were one. Even from a distance, she could tell he loved horses.

Suddenly Chance looked toward the house, then he tilted his head toward the second floor. To the windows where she was standing. Joy started to step back out of his sight. She didn't want him to know she'd been watching him. But when his gaze caught hers, she froze. She couldn't even breathe as his eyes held her prisoner. Finally one of the other men called for his attention.

Joy closed her eyes and drew in a needed breath. She was in trouble. Big trouble.

"That was the best pot roast I've ever eaten," Hank announced from his seat at the head of the dining-room table.

"I second that," Chance said as other accolades came from the three neighboring ranchers who'd been invited to supper.

"Well, thank you," Joy said. "I haven't cooked in a while, so I am a little rusty. Besides, Ella helped a lot."

Ella brought more rolls to the table. "All I did was watch Katie."

"And you did a good job," Hank announced. "We'll have you babysit whenever Joy comes by again."

Ella placed her hands on her hips. "If that's your way of telling me my cooking isn't as good as Joy's, I already know that. But I never noticed you turning down one of my meals Hank Barrett," she snapped before she marched into the kitchen.

The table grew silent. Joy started to get up and see if Ella was all right. Hank placed his hand over hers.

"I'll go," he said. "Since I'm the one who hurt her feelings." He excused himself and disappeared into the kitchen.

"I'm sorry," Joy said to Chance. "I didn't mean to cause any trouble."

Chance smiled. "You didn't. Hank and Ella have these fights at least once a week. He usually says something that sets her off. Your cooking tonight had nothing to do with it.'' His hand reached for hers.

"Are you sure?'' she asked.

Chance nodded, not wanting to release her hand. His excuse was that they were newlyweds and people expected them to act the part. That included all the touching…the kissing. He was taking advantage, but he couldn't seem to help himself. "I'm sure.'' He leaned closer and touched his lips to hers. He felt her intake of breath, then when he pulled away, he saw the desire in her eyes, and nearly lost it.

"After dessert I'll take you out to see the new colt.''

He watched her nod, then she got up from the table. "I'll go cut the pie.''

Angry with himself for his weakness, Chance watched her leave. He needed to handle this better. Joy Spencer only wanted a business relationship, not a marriage. But damn, how was he going to keep his hands off her?

Thirty minutes later, while Hank helped Ella with the dishes, Chance walked Joy across the yard toward the barn.

"It must have been nice growing up here,'' she said.

"My brothers and I didn't think so at the time, but looking back, coming to live with Hank was the best thing that happened to us.''

Joy could only imagine how devastating it had been for three adolescent boys to have their whole world torn apart, and to carry the stigma of their father's sins for years. Was that the reason Cade and Travis left home?

"What about your brothers? Are they in ranching, too?''

He shook his head. "Cade went off to college in

Chicago. Now, he's some hotshot financial analyst for a big investment firm there. Travis is in Houston. He has his own computer security company."

"You must be proud of them."

He nodded. "Sure am."

"But you miss them."

Chance didn't answer, but she saw the pain in his eyes.

"Hey, how about you?" he asked. "Have you always lived in Denver?"

"No, my parents divorced when I was five. My mom and I moved around a lot. That's why I'm so adamant about Katie having a permanent home."

Chance knew his life hadn't been perfect, but from the time he'd been fourteen, he'd had Hank. He still had Hank—and his brothers.

"Do you have any brothers or sisters?" he asked.

"No. Just me and my mom. I never got to see my dad much."

"I'm sorry, Joy." He held open the barn door, and they stepped inside.

"My life wasn't that bad," she assured him. "Maybe a little lonely."

Chance had been lucky; no matter how bad it had gotten, he'd always had his brothers, Hank and Ella and the ranch.

They walked down the center aisle as the familiar scents of fresh hay and horses teased his nostrils. At the last stall, he opened the gate, went inside and began to soothe the mare, then crooned to the jumpy colt in the corner.

"Oh, he's beautiful, Chance," Joy said as she joined him. Kneeling down in the straw, she coaxed the curious colt to come to her. He remained just out of reach.

"This is Stormy Night."

"Well, hello, Stormy." Joy let the colt see her hand. Chance liked the way she acted around the animal. No fear, just total confidence that she would be accepted. It worked. The colt came closer and let her stroke his head.

"Well, I'll be darned," Chance said. "He's never let anyone get close to him."

Joy smiled. "It's this universal mother thing."

"You're just a charmer."

Her blue eyes met his in question. "What?"

"You turned on your charm, he couldn't resist. Like every man at the dinner table tonight couldn't take their eyes off you." It had worked on him as well. "I guess it works on my horses, too."

"I wasn't trying to attract attention. Did I do something that was out of place?"

"Oh, no." He released the mare and went to her. "I was teasing, Joy. You're new around here, and people are curious about you—about us. I mean, we married pretty fast."

"Oh, Chance. I guess I didn't think about the trouble this would cause you."

He gripped her shoulders. "No, Joy. I'm not sorry. I'm glad they like you. I like you."

She looked up at him, her blue eyes rich with color. "I like you, too."

They stood there, unmoving. It would be so easy just to lean down and kiss her, he thought. Chance had never wanted anything more. He ached to. He weakened and drew her closer. "Oh, Joy," he breathed her name. "You wouldn't like me if you knew what I was thinking right now."

Her hands moved to his chest. "What are you thinking?"

"How much I want to kiss you."

She swallowed hard as a blush rose to her cheeks. "You do?"

Chance groaned his desire as his head descended toward hers, but the sudden sound of voices coming into the barn broke the spell. Joy tried to pull away, but he refused to allow her escape. He held her close, revelling in the feel of her body against his. "It's okay, Joy. We're married."

Still she pushed at his chest until he released her.

"I've got to go to Katie," she said and hurried out of the stall.

Before he could stop her, Hank appeared along with Matt Henson, Bob Hicks and Harlin Graff, the neighboring ranchers.

"I couldn't talk these guys into staying up at the house," Hank said. "So I'm taking them to get settled in the bunkhouse."

"We just want to play a few hands of poker before we turn in," Bob Hicks said. "Don't get many boys' nights out these days. But I doubt we'll have the pleasure of Chance's company this year. Not with his pretty new bride. How come you aren't chasing after that pretty filly?"

Chance wasn't listening to the men's kidding. His thoughts were on Joy, but he doubted she wanted anything to do with him. "I'll be staying in the bunkhouse myself," he announced as he closed the gate.

He got frowns from all the men, then Hank spoke.

"I don't think anyone expects you to, Chance. You should stay at the house with Joy and Katie."

Harlin spoke up. "My Margie would skin me alive if I chose staying with the men over her. Besides, the men will never let you live it down if you show up in the bunkhouse."

"I just thought it would be more convenient," Chance offered, knowing he would be in for an earful of kidding from the hands. But if he showed up in the bedroom Joy would be upset, especially after what had nearly happened. She wouldn't trust him within ten feet of her. And she shouldn't. But he couldn't let anyone know their marriage was only pretend. He looked at Hank. "I'll be down here at five for breakfast."

Chance wandered off to the bunkhouse and grabbed his duffel bag from his bunk while several of the men teased him. He accepted the good-natured kidding, then left for the house. Passing through the kitchen he said good-night to Ella and went up the stairs. On the second floor, he gripped the brass doorknob to his bedroom and drew a long breath before going inside.

"Joy," he whispered. The room was dark except for the moonlight coming through the windows, silhouetting his wife sitting in the rocking chair, feeding the baby.

"Chance!" she gasped. "What are you doing here?"

He closed the door behind him and leaned against it. "It looks like I'll be sleeping in here tonight."

Joy held Katie against her breast, soothing her. She knew that the darkness shielded her in privacy, but there was something unsettling about Chance being so near.

"There isn't room in the bunkhouse?" she asked.

"Yes, but the men chased me up here," he said. "How could I tell them I couldn't sleep with my wife?" He went to the bed, pulled off the blanket and a pillow. "Don't worry, I'll sleep on the floor."

She glanced over her shoulder as Chance went to the far wall and tossed his bedding down. "You can't sleep there. You have to be on a horse all day tomorrow. You take the bed."

He moved to the closet and opened it. He pulled off his boots and began stripping off his shirt. "I'm not taking the bed from you."

Next came his belt. Even in the moonlight she could see the enormous width of his shoulders. He turned to her, exposing his muscular chest and flat stomach. Her breath caught as he came closer.

"You need your rest, too, Joy," he said. "I've slept on the ground before."

"But I can sleep here. In this chair."

He glanced at Katie, and Joy knew he could see her exposed breast. His piercing gaze made her blood surge. "I can't let you do that."

"But Katie will be waking up during the night anyway."

He knelt down beside the chair, his hand brushing the child's head, just inches from her breast. "Then we'll both wake up, but you're going to be sleeping in the bed."

Stubborn man. "Then you're going to be sleeping there, too." She watched his eyes narrow. "I mean, it's a large bed. I don't see anything wrong with you sleeping on top of the covers—on your side."

He drew a breath. "Lady, you're playing with fire."

She remembered all too well what had nearly happened in the barn. "Not if we don't let anything happen. All I'm offering you, Chance, is one side of a bed. Nothing more."

He watched her for what seemed like an eternity, then said, "I'll take it." He got up, retrieved the blanket and pillow and, leaving on his jeans, lay down on top of the bed.

Joy released a long breath, praying she hadn't made a mistake. She looked heavenward and prayed, *Please, don't let me need him. Don't let me care for him.*

Chance lay perfectly still as Joy curled against his chest. Her hand snaked out and caressed his already sensitized skin, her fingers finding their way through the hair on his chest. In seconds, she had him hot and hard and wanting her so badly he had to clench his fists to keep from touching her. Then she moved her leg against his, and he bit his lip to keep from groaning.

Damn, he was dying here.

Thank God, he had on his jeans. He opened his eyes to glance at the clock. It was nearly five o'clock. He needed to get up. That meant he had to wake Joy.

He gripped her arm. "Come on, blue eyes," he whispered, hoping she'd move away and he could slip out of bed. But no such luck. She only scooted closer, her hand hugging him. Then with a throaty groan, her lips trailed across his chest.

He couldn't take any more. "Joy," he said again, then shook her hard.

She raised her head and blinked at him. Her heavy-lidded eyes looked into his, but he doubted he was the source of her desire. She was probably thinking of her husband.

"Chance…"

"I need to get going," he said.

"Oh, my," she gasped and moved away. "I'm sorry, I didn't mean to…"

"Sshh." He placed a finger over her lips. "It's okay. I understand," he said. But if he didn't get out of this bed, he wouldn't be responsible for what happened. "Now, I need to shower and get down to the bunkhouse." He grabbed his bag and headed for the bathroom. "A long cold one," he whispered after he closed the door.

Ten minutes later, Chance came out to find Joy dressed in her robe. She was standing at the windows, the morning sun haloing her blond head. "Do you want me to fix you some breakfast?" she asked.

He stood rooted to the spot, afraid of getting too close to her. "No, we hired a cook for the men. Just concentrate on that fried chicken of yours."

She smiled, and his heart ended up in his throat. "I hope you're not disappointed."

Nothing about her could ever disappoint him. And what he had in mind was going to get him in trouble. "I'm not worried. We'll be bringing in the herd from the north pasture about one o'clock. Just have lunch ready."

"I've never seen a roundup before, I'll be there waiting for you."

Before Chance allowed himself to read more into Joy's words, he grabbed his boots and walked out, telling himself he would be crazy to start dreaming of something he could never have.

He was Joy Spencer Randell's temporary husband, nothing more.

* * *

Chance stretched in the saddle as he let his horse take the lead and keep the herd on course. It was a good thing Ace knew the way, because he hadn't been able to keep his mind on anything all morning. Thanks to Joy, all he'd done was relive what had happened in bed this morning. How she'd felt in his arms. How much he wanted her.

He glanced up as they approached the ranch and the branding pens behind the corral. Chance wondered if she would really be there.

"Getting anxious to see that bride of yours?" Harlin asked as he rode up next to him.

Chance wanted more than just the sight of Joy. "That and some coffee."

The middle-aged man grinned. "Your new missus seems awful nice. Not hard on the eyes, either."

Nobody had to tell Chance how beautiful Joy was. He caught himself staring at her all the time. "She's that all right."

"You're a good man, Chance Randell. Not many men would take on a ready-made family."

"I'm the lucky one. Katie Rose is just a wonderful bonus."

Harlin nodded to the pens off in the distance. "Well, looks like you're going to see both of them real soon."

Joy stood shielding her eyes from the sun. Ella had insisted she wear a hat and had found her an old Stetson to keep the sun off her face. She was wearing the only jeans that fit her, except for the top button, and she'd found a chambray shirt in Chance's closet that she wore over a white T-shirt, helping to hide her still-thick waist.

"They're coming," one of the women called from the other side of the corral.

"C'mon, Joy. Let's get a closer look." Ella pulled her to the pen's railing. "Climb up."

Joy climbed up to the second rung and looked at the small cloud of dust ahead. Eight men on horseback came into view. Her gaze danced from one to the other, trying to find Chance.

All at once, she spotted him. His size and broad shoulders were hard to miss. Back straight, he looked more comfortable on a horse than anywhere else. He rode closer, and she felt her excitement grow.

The sound of bawling calves grew louder as the pen was opened and cows and bulls were separated. Chance had his black hat pulled low and a lasso in his gloved hand as he drove the huge bulls into a large pen. Joy glanced at the intimidating animals, then turned back to the small calves, crying for their mothers as they were herded into a different area.

It took about twenty minutes for the task to be completed, then the men got off their horses and came to greet their wives. Chance was one of the last to climb down off his horse. As he walked toward Joy, his gait was sure and direct. He wore brown leather chaps that didn't hide the strength of his long legs. He was the ultimate working cowboy.

His light-gray gaze was on her as he made his way in her direction.

Joy felt her panic build as his gaze locked with hers. He started across the pen, and something in his dangerous look told her to beware.

"Well howdy there, cowgirl," he said, eyeing her outfit.

"Hi," she answered and glanced down at her tennis shoes. "Not exactly appropriate for the day."

He pulled off his hat, allowing sandy brown hair to fall across his forehead. He looked ten years younger. "We'll have to fix that the next time we go into town. Every cowgirl needs boots." He wrapped his arms around her. "But right now, I better kiss you hello." He cocked his head to the men behind him, and whispered, "Wouldn't want them to think anything's wrong."

This morning she'd crawled all over him like some wanton woman. How could she deny him a kiss? And if she were honest, she didn't want to deny herself. "We wouldn't want that to happen," she said, realizing she was trembling.

He drew her close. "Easy, blue eyes, I promise this isn't going to hurt a bit."

Slowly his mouth descended to hers, touching her lips tentatively, pulling back, then coming back for another taste. Joy whimpered, wanting more, needing more. He accommodated her, his mouth covering hers in a hungry kiss, then he pushed his tongue inside, tasting her thoroughly, leaving no doubt of his desire.

Skyrockets shot off in Joy's head as he swept her away to a time and place for just the two of them. It had been so long since she'd felt this need…a man's closeness…longing.

Suddenly the sounds of whistles and catcalls brought her back to reality. Chance drew back, but his eyes remained fixed on her, ignoring everyone else.

He reached up and straightened her hat. "Oh, lady, I like the way you say hello." He took a breath. "I guess that should convince them."

"Yeah," she answered, breathless and sorry it was over.

Chapter Eight

As promised, Joy had worked hard all morning preparing her chicken. Thank goodness she'd had help from the bunkhouse cook, Jerry, plus Ella and three of the ranchers' wives. Of course, that had been in between the women taking turns holding Katie.

But Joy had made good on her promise to Chance and had fried chicken. Actually it was grilled, but under the circumstances, it was the best she could do. To simplify things, Joy had used the huge outdoor barbecue to grill the dozens of pieces. While she'd supervised, Jerry did the actual cooking of her spicy marinated chicken. Tables had been set up for the ranch hands, and were laden with the other food, including baked beans, potato salad and coleslaw. The hard work had been worth it. The men came back for seconds, including Chance. She was still dishing out pieces when he came back through the line.

"You make the best chicken I've ever eaten."

"Why thank you, Mr. Randell." She smiled

sweetly, enjoying the teasing. "I'm glad you're pleased. What can I get you, a leg or a breast?" Her face flamed, but seeing the glint in his eyes made her body tingle.

"That's a hard decision since yours are the best I've ever tasted."

Hearing the huskiness in Chance's voice, she couldn't seem to draw air into her lungs.

"How about I sample both?" he said.

Somehow Joy managed to maneuver the tongs and placed two pieces on his plate. He winked, leaving her wondering about more than just his preference in chicken.

Two hours later, Chance was dirty and sweaty, and more tired than he could ever remember. His lack of sleep last night was beginning to take its toll. And he wasn't done yet. There were still a couple dozen calves to brand, inoculate and castrate. And tomorrow was another day. They had to bring in another herd.

He couldn't help but wonder how Joy was taking her first roundup. Most city women didn't like to see this side of ranching. But raising cattle was a business and the livelihood of the Circle B. Cattle weren't pets. So if Joy planned to live on a ranch, she'd have to get used to it.

He shot the inoculation gun into the bawling calf's hip. He and Harlin released the animal, and he went running off to his mama. Chance looked toward the fence and found Joy watching him. How long had she been there? He called over another hand to take his place and wandered over to her.

"Want to help?" he teased.

She shook her head. "I'll just watch. It's pretty gruesome."

"It's ranch life, Joy. If you want to live here, this is all a part of it. These animals provide those wonderful steaks we enjoy eating."

"I know." She took a breath and released it. "But it still must be hard to know they're going off to the slaughterhouse."

Chance shrugged. "I guess I'm used to it." He glanced around at the busy activity. Every man had a job. A roper on horseback swung a lasso over his head, then with an expert flip of his wrist, caught a calf's hind legs. With the help of his well-trained horse, he dragged the animal to the branding area, where one of the hands branded, while another inoculated, and another castrated the bull calves. With the men working in unison, it was all over in minutes.

"I guess I'll get used to it too, someday."

Joy's words made him smile. "It'll take time, but you can do it."

She eyed him closely. "I bet you're tired. You couldn't have gotten much sleep last night...with Katie crying and all."

"I wouldn't have gotten much more in the bunkhouse. These roundups are like a long party. So don't worry about it."

"But I do."

He came closer to the fence. She looked so cute in her jeans and his shirt. Her hat was a little big and sat cockeyed on her head. "Last night wasn't so bad. The best sleep I had was when you were all curled up in my arms." He knew he shouldn't say it, but he couldn't seem to keep the words locked inside.

He watched her swallow hard. "But we shouldn't…"

"Shouldn't what? All we did was sleep together. *Sleep*. If anything else were to go on, believe me, blue eyes, I'd make sure you weren't complaining about it the next morning." Before he said anything more foolish, he swung around and walked back to the branding, knowing tonight he'd be lucky if she let him in the bedroom, much less the bed.

That evening, after assigning jobs to the hands for tomorrow's drive, Chance made his way up to the bedroom. When he opened the door, Joy sat in the rocking chair, holding Katie. He'd tried to wait downstairs to give mother and child some privacy, but everyone had turned in.

"Sorry, I thought you'd have finished feeding her."

Joy glanced over her shoulder. "I have, she's almost asleep."

He nodded. "I'll just go take a shower." He took off his boots and walked to the closet. Opening the door, he discovered Joy's clothes were hanging next to his. His hand brushed her robe, the silkiness sliding over his fingertips like a caress.

He couldn't even handle her clothes without feeling a surge of desire. What was he going to do with her in bed again?

He heard Katie whimper and turned around. Standing, Joy placed the baby against her shoulder and started walking her.

"Is she okay?" he asked in a whispered voice.

The baby cried louder. "Just too many people handling her today." Even in the dim light, he could see the tired look on Joy's face.

"Here. Let me take her for a while." Before she could protest, he lifted the tiny infant from her arms. "I'll settle her down. Why don't you go take a shower or a bath if you like. I'll take care of her."

"But, I can't…"

"Yes, you can," he argued. "You've worked hard today, too. Wouldn't you like thirty minutes to yourself?"

She sighed. "Oh, that sounds heavenly."

"Then go." He walked toward the closet, reached in and handed her her robe. "Go. I'll have this one asleep before you finish."

She gathered her things, then started for the door. "I forgot to change her diaper."

"I can handle it," he lied.

Joy finally left him and the crying Katie alone. He cradled her against his shoulder. "Hey, little one, you're making me look bad in front of your mother. Let's have some cooperation here." He placed her down on the bed and found the diaper bag. He took out a disposable diaper and examined its tiny shape. This was supposed to go on the baby? Taking a container of wipes, he returned to the bawling Katie. She had kicked away her gown exposing her legs.

"C'mon, sweetheart, give a guy a break here," he crooned as he lifted the baby's gown higher, took hold of her legs and raised them, removing the wet diaper. As quickly as he could, he wiped the tiny bottom, then taped a dry diaper in place, all the time trying to soothe the upset child.

Finally he hoisted Katie to his shoulder and began patting her back. "Now, doesn't that feel better?" he said. A few tiny sobs escaped, then came a big yawn.

Chance began to hum a country-and-western song.

He felt silly, but it seemed to work. Katie remained quiet. Continuing to walk around the room with his precious cargo, he wandered to the windows and looked out at the moonlit night. The lights in the bunkhouse were out. He smiled to himself, knowing how hard the men had worked today. They weren't interested in anything but sleep.

Chance wished that were true for him. He turned in the direction of the connecting bathroom, hearing the water run. Joy was in the tub. He could picture her with her head leaning back against the edge, her eyes closed…and gloriously, sinfully naked.

Damn. He had to stop thinking about her. He was walking a dangerous line here. And after that kiss today, he couldn't think straight. *Well, you have to get Joy out of your mind,* he told himself. *This isn't a real marriage, so don't get all excited.*

Katie jerked against his shoulder, and he rubbed her back again. Finally she quieted enough to put her down. But the second he took her from his shoulder, she began to fuss, so he carried her around for a while longer. Finally, exhausted, Chance sat down on the bed, then stretched out, allowing Katie to curl up against his chest. He would close his eyes…just for a minute.

Joy checked her hair in the mirror again, knowing she was stalling. She didn't want to leave the safety of the bathroom. But she knew she had to. She couldn't sleep in here. She glanced around the small room, realizing she was seriously considering it.

"You chicken. You can't keep avoiding the man forever. He's your husband." She leaned against the sink. No, he wasn't. Blake was her husband, her only true husband. It was best she remember that. But after the kiss she'd shared with Chance today, it was getting harder. She just had to stay away from the man.

Joy pulled open the door and entered the silent bedroom. She glanced at the bed and found Chance. Joy's heart tightened when she saw Katie curled up on his chest. They were both sound asleep. Walking to the bed, Joy couldn't take her eyes off the touching scene. Katie was lying peacefully on her stomach with her little bottom sticking up in the air.

"You're a fraud, Chance Randell. That tough-guy image is all an act."

Careful not to disturb either Katie or Chance, she lifted her daughter into her arms. Immediately, Chance jumped and reach for her.

"Katie," he whispered.

Joy smiled at his protectiveness. "I've got her," Joy told him. "I'll put her to bed."

After tucking Katie into her crib, Joy returned to the bed. "Looks like you worked your special magic."

"She just wanted to be held."

Don't we all, Joy thought. "You'd better get some sleep." She walked around to the other side of the bed and pulled back the blanket. "You have another full day tomorrow."

He swung his legs off the bed and began stripping off his shirt. "Don't remind me." He looked at her, his gray eyes glassy. "Is it okay for me to sleep on the bed?"

Nodding, she felt her throat tighten as she looked at his bare chest. "I promise I won't attack you again. I mean I usually don't…"

He shook his head. "Hey, did I complain?" He

tossed his shirt in the corner and removed his belt. "Besides, all you did was curl up next to me."

Joy shut her eyes, feeling the blush climb up her face. "Right, that's all."

He returned to the bed and stretched out on top of the blanket. Without so much as a good-night, the man fell asleep. All Joy heard was the soft sound of his snoring. It kept her awake...for a long time.

The next day was just as long and tiring, but Chance welcomed the hard physical work. He ached all over from being in the saddle a second day. Joy had stayed away from the pens during the branding part of the day. He'd heard that she was busy in the kitchen helping Ella with the food. That was for the best, but that hadn't stopped him from looking for her, wanting her there.

That evening he barely made it through supper. All he wanted to do was sleep. He waited until Joy fed Katie, then he fell into bed and that was all he remembered. The next morning, he awoke and found Joy way over on her side of the bed. He ached to reach for her and pull her into his arms. But instead, he got up and went to take a shower.

After dressing, he went down to the bunkhouse and ate breakfast with the men. Once again they were harassing him about sleeping at the house.

"Wouldn't you if you had a beautiful wife?" he said jokingly. He finished his coffee and went to saddle his horse. He wanted to start the day and stop thinking about Joy. Stop thinking about how sweet she smelled first thing in the morning, or how soft her skin was, or how pretty she looked every waking hour of the day.

Chance opened the gate to Ace's stall carrying his tack. He rubbed the horse's nose and proceeded to saddle him. Then Chance led the buckskin out to the corral where the others had gathered.

Checking the straps again, he climbed into the saddle for the last day of the roundup. If there were no complications, they should be finished today. After the barbecue tonight, everyone could go home. Joy and he would return to the ranch and things would go back to as before. She would sleep in her bedroom, and he would be in his down the hall.

Was that what he wanted? After three days of being close to Joy, could he go back? *Hell, buddy, it isn't your choice to make,* he reminded himself.

He glanced up to the house. The sun was just peeking over the horizon as his gaze went to his bedroom windows. There was a light on and more than that. He found Joy standing in the window. Still dressed in her gown and robe, her hair was wild around her face. She looked beautiful.

One of the men rode up beside him. "I guess Mrs. Randell forgot to say good-bye."

Chance nodded, fighting to keep from getting down from his horse and giving her a proper greeting. He shook away the thought. He had to think about business. Not just their agreement. He had a roundup to finish.

"C'mon, let's get going," he called to the men on horseback. The men whooped with excitement as they started for the gate.

Chance stole one last glance at his wife. He couldn't help but wish things were different. He took the reins and rode after the men, knowing from past experience that he was dreaming a fool's dream. But it was too late.

Joy sank down on the bed, glad of a few minutes to relax. Between taking care of Katie and helping Ella with the meal for the barbecue tonight, she hadn't had a moment to herself. The roundup was officially over today, and they always celebrated with a party. The families of the men helping out were also invited to the barbecue and dance. Hank was going all out for tonight. He was barbecuing steaks and had even hired a band.

Joy was looking forward to the festivities, because when they were over, she and Chance would be going home and things would get back to normal. That was good. They wouldn't have to pretend anymore. Chance's kisses would end, and she'd be sleeping in her own bed, alone. A pang of disappointment surged through her when she realized they'd return to being polite strangers.

Was that what they were? she wondered. She found she liked sharing her days and nights with another person. Not just anyone. Chance Randell—the brooding cowboy who'd stormed into her life bent on rescuing her. How had he come to be so dear to her? Lying back on the bed, Joy allowed the tears to fill her eyes. She couldn't let herself fall for any man. Somehow she always ended up getting hurt. First her father had left her, then she'd lost Blake. She couldn't stand it happening again. No. She refused to fall in love again.

The bedroom door opened and Chance walked in. Joy brushed away the tears, not wanting him to see her like this.

"Joy, are you all right?" Dressed in jeans and a

Western shirt, still wearing his leather chaps, he came
to her side and knelt down.

She nodded, seeing the concern in his gray eyes.
"Yes, just one of those hormonal moments. I feel so
foolish." He was too close, and she stood up. "Just a
rough morning."

"Well, we'll be home tomorrow," he said, coming
up behind her. "Things will be back to normal."

After their closeness the past few days, Joy doubted
things would be the same again. "I've been missing
the ranch, too, and Sunny and Ginger. I hope the
Campbells will be willing to give them back."

"The pups probably miss you, too." His eyes
searched her face. "I'm sorry, this roundup has been
hard on you."

She shook her head. "No, it's been wonderful. It's
the most fun I've had in a long time." She looked
down at her hands. "It's just all this pretending…it's
been hard." Joy glanced up in time to see a flash of
pain in his eyes, and how quickly he masked it.

"Well, it will be over soon," he said. "If you're
too tired, you can skip the barbecue. People will understand."

"Oh, no, Chance, I want to go. I've met so many
nice people. I'm fine, really."

He didn't look convinced. He took a peek at Katie
sleeping in the crib. "Then take a nap for a while."

She nodded.

"I need to finish up some things at the pens. I'll be
gone for another hour. Will you be all right?"

"Of course. I've been on my own for a long time."

"That doesn't mean I can't worry about you."

She smiled. "I'll be better after I rest."

To her surprise his hand reached out and stroked

her cheek. She fought to keep herself from swaying into his touch. "Make sure you do," he said. He turned and left, leaving Joy wanting more. More, she knew, than she could ever have.

By nine o'clock that evening, the band was in full swing, and the concrete patio was crowded with people two-stepping. The neighboring ranchers were all in attendance, enjoying the excuse to have a party.

"This gets better every year," Hank said, talking over the loud music.

"We're lucky to get so much free help," Chance said.

"Son, this help isn't free. We'll be helping the other ranchers for the next month. But I was worried about you handling the load, with Joy and Katie. I mean, it was easy to send you off to work roundups when you were single. But now things are different."

Things weren't that different, Chance thought. "I won't go on any long-distance ones. Not when Katie's so little."

Hank smiled. "I wouldn't want to leave those two beauties for long, either." He placed a hand on Chance's shoulder. "Marriage seems to agree with you. Everything seems to be working out."

Chance nodded. What could he say to Hank? That he and his wife were two strangers living together?

"I wish your brothers would settle down, too. Of course, I'd want them to settle down right here in San Angelo."

"I sure could go for a visit from them," Chance said, knowing both of them were wishing for something that probably wouldn't happen. Cade and Travis had taken a lot of abuse from people who hated what their father had done. Chance had toughed it out and survived, but his brothers found that college out of the area provided an escape. "I'm going to try and coax them home this summer. Maybe for your birthday."

The older man frowned. "I'm not having any more birthdays."

Chance grinned. "That's right, this is the big one. Sixty-five. What does that make you, a senior citizen?"

"Watch your mouth, boy, I can still pin your ears back."

Chance didn't doubt it for a moment. "I think I'll go find Joy." He wandered off through the crowd and finally spotted her talking with some of the ladies who'd helped with the cooking.

He was taken aback by how lovely she looked. Her fitted pink T-shirt showed off her small build and full breasts. The floral skirt hugged a slimming waist and draped nicely to mid-calf. Her long hair was pinned back, leaving blond curls around her shoulders. She turned to him and her eyes sparkled with excitement.

"Having fun?" he asked.

She smiled. "Yes. Everyone is so nice."

"Good. How about a dance?"

"Oh, I haven't danced in years."

He gave her the once-over. "It will come back to you."

"Really, I'm not very good at the two-step."

"Then you can stumble through it with me." He placed his hand against the small of her back and guided her toward the dance floor. "Who's watching Katie?"

"She's sleeping. Ella is taking the first shift until I have to feed her."

He drew her into his arms in the middle of the floor, so as not to disturb the faster, more experienced dancers. He started with slow steps, and when she began to follow his lead, he picked up the pace. Soon they were both in time with the music.

"See, you're a natural." He spun her out, and she giggled when she landed back in his arms.

The tune ended and a ballad began to play. There were no words exchanged between them as Chance pulled Joy into his arms. A dozen sensations bombarded him at once as they began to move around the dance floor.

Joy was all woman. Her softness against him made it difficult for Chance to breathe. But who needed air? He tightened his hold, and when she didn't resist, he rested his chin against her hair. She smelled so sweet. Her scent was intoxicating.

He danced her to the edge of the patio. The light was dim and the noisy crowd and music faded away, but he continued to sway with her in his arms. It all felt so right, so perfect. Finally the music ended and Chance raised his head, but didn't release her.

"That was nice," he managed to say.

"Yes, nice," she breathed.

"My favorite part is holding you in my arms."

She started to glance away, but his fingers touched her face and drew her gaze back to his. "I liked us being close these past few days. I think you liked it, too." His voice was a ragged whisper as he searched her eyes. Seeing the flash of her desire, he felt he'd been tossed a lifeline.

"We can't do anything about it," she said weakly.

"You can't deny that something's going on between us."

Chance circled her neck with one hand and took her inviting mouth, not giving himself a chance to think about the consequences. His kiss was raw and demanding, not the kind a woman like Joy was accustomed to. But he soon discovered she was just as eager, so ready to kiss him back that it made him hungrier for her. He drew her against him as his tongue delved inside, unable to get enough of her sweet taste, the smell of her and the feel of her. Deepening the kiss, he swallowed her moan of satisfaction as he pressed his body to hers, trying to get closer.

It wasn't enough, he wanted more. He needed more. He tore his mouth from hers. "Oh, blue eyes, I want you…"

He heard the catch in her breath. "No, Chance, I can't…I had a baby…."

"I know, but that doesn't stop the ache…."

Before Joy could say any more, Ella called out. Joy pulled away quickly as the housekeeper approached them. "I'm sorry to spoil your evening, but your daughter is hungry."

Joy lowered her gaze shyly as she pushed her hair behind her ears. "It's time I fed her," she said and started after Ella.

Chance didn't want their time together to end. "I'll go with you," he offered.

Joy released a sigh. "Chance, I think it would be best if I went up alone. We both need time…to cool off."

Before he could protest, she turned and left him standing there. He began to pace, Joy's words eating at his gut like acid. Cool off? She had kissed him until he couldn't think a rational thought, then told him to go and cool off.

The pain from Joy's rejection was like a knife in his heart. The blue-eyed city woman had gotten to him, Chance thought, feeling his protective wall tumbling down. Hell, he should have known better. How many times did he need to be socked in the gut before it would sink in?

Women like Joy Spencer didn't take up with a Randell.

Chapter Nine

Joy hadn't been surprised when the party ended that Chance packed up the truck right away. He seemed eager to get her and Katie home. They rode back to the ranch in silence, and things didn't change once they arrived at the ranch.

It was after midnight before Joy got Katie settled down. Exhausted herself, she fell into bed, only hearing the click of Chance's bedroom door as she drifted off.

By 6:00 a.m. the next morning, Joy had fed Katie and was coming downstairs to make breakfast for Chance and discuss what had happened last night. She walked into the kitchen to find her husband seated at the table, an empty cereal bowl evidence that he'd already eaten.

She hid her disappointment. "If you give me a few minutes, I can fix you some eggs." She went to the stove and pulled out a skillet.

"I'm fine." He took a sip of his coffee.

Good, then they could talk. Joy got herself some coffee and sat down at the table. "Chance, about last night..."

The scraping of his chair as Chance stood drowned out anything else Joy was going to say. "I'll be working in the barn this morning." He went to the sink and dumped the remainder of his coffee in the sink, then started out.

Joy's mouth dropped in surprise as she watched him put on his cowboy hat. "Wait," she called. "You aren't even going to talk to me?"

He met her with a stony gaze. "What's to talk about? You made yourself clear last night." He stood there for a moment, then turned to walk out.

"Chance." She caught up with him on the porch. "There's plenty to talk about. Why I thought it was better that—"

"Don't, Joy," he said, and shut his eyes momentarily. "You made yourself clear on how you feel last night."

She swallowed, wishing she could say just the right thing to make it all go away. But she saw by the stubborn set of his jaw, he wasn't going to listen. "So this is how it's going to be?"

"You made up the rules, I just follow them." With that he walked off toward the barn.

It wasn't until after eight o'clock that evening that Chance returned to the house. Before Joy could tell him his supper was in the oven, he told her he was tired and went upstairs to shower...then into his room. She didn't see him the rest of the night.

Joy got the message loud and clear, Chance didn't want to talk. Talk about what? A few kisses? Admit that they wanted each other? It was only natural.

They'd been thrown together for days. And Chance Randell was an attractive man. Her thoughts went to Blake. Her dear, sweet husband. Their four-year marriage had been a comfortable union. Lovemaking hadn't caused much in the fireworks department, but it had been satisfying. She'd been happy.

Now, just Chance's presence threatened that memory. The night of the barbecue, Joy hadn't wanted to face the fact that her feelings for Chance had changed. It terrified her to think she was wanting more than a pretend marriage. A taste of what life could be with Chance was becoming too real.

Joy walked back into the kitchen. No, she had to push him away. She wouldn't risk her heart again. Katie was the only one she could think about now. She needed to give her daughter a good, loving home, away from the Spencers. Her thoughts turned to Chance and how, from the beginning, he had always been there for her. How he'd made her feel safe. Oh, why did everything have to get so complicated?

In her solitude, Joy stayed busy with Katie, and while her daughter napped she cleaned and polished the house from top to bottom. Then in the warm afternoons, she took Katie outside and started weeding the flowerbeds. She pruned the neglected roses, even spread some fertilizer. On a trip into town, she stopped at the nursery for some bedding plants, adding color to the edge of the porch.

But nothing changed the fact that Chance was still avoiding her. He was gone before she came downstairs in the mornings, and didn't return to the house until supper. His hard work was paying off, though. The place was looking wonderful. But she missed the man she used to share things with.

She and Chance might be living under the same roof, but there hadn't been any real communication between them since they'd left the Circle B nearly two weeks ago. Even Katie seemed to be aware of the change. Joy had to do something to get them back to where things were before. But could they go back to a business relationship? If she stepped over that line, there would be no going back. And she didn't know if she was ready yet. If she'd ever be.

The following Monday, Joy needed to go into town for her six-week doctor's visit. But Ella wasn't able to watch Katie. That meant Joy had to reschedule or ask Chance.

She went out to the barn. When she stepped inside she inhaled the scent of fresh-cut wood. At the sound of hammering coming from the back, she made her way down the center aisle, eagerly taking in all the changes. The place had been cleaned, stalls repaired, some just with a few slats replaced; others had new gates and hinges. Four new stalls had also been built.

She couldn't help but feel excited knowing there would be horses soon. When she reached the last stall she found Chance working inside. He was shirtless, and the muscles across his sweat-glistened back bunched as he hammered a nail into a board. She admired how his jeans pulled taut across his narrow hips and thighs as he knelt down to guide another board into place. Her heart skipped a beat, remembering the power of this man, also how gentle he could be to Katie…to her.

He sensed her presence and turned around. There was a look of surprise, then his eyes narrowed in question. "You need something?" He stood and came to her.

She was hurt by his abruptness. "A favor. I have to go into town to the doctor's. I know you're busy, but could you watch Katie for a few hours? She's sleeping now, and maybe she'll sleep the whole time I'm gone, but if not, I left a bottle in the refrigerator." Joy knew she was rambling, but she couldn't help herself. This glaring man wasn't cutting her any slack. "Never mind, I'll just take her with me." Sad that their relationship had come to this, she started to leave.

"I'll watch her," Chance said and grabbed his shirt off the railing.

"You sure?"

He nodded and slipped it on. "I could use a break," he said. "I'll just do some paperwork at the house."

"Paperwork? You have paperwork?"

They walked out of the barn and into the bright sunlight. "When you run a ranch you need to keep track of your livestock. Even records of the trees in your pecan orchard."

Joy had no idea there was so much involved in running a ranch.

They reached the steps and were greeted by Ginger and Sunny leashed in the yard. Chance petted both puppies, and Joy felt a twinge of jealousy at the attention he gave them.

He stepped up on the porch and turned toward her. His shirt was hanging open and Joy was drawn to his perfectly sculptured chest. Her fingertips tingled to reach out and touch him, to feel the muscles beneath his skin. Her gaze went to his face and found his cold look.

"I'll be back as soon as I can," she said. "You sure you'll be all right?"

"If you don't trust me to watch Katie, why did you ask?"

"I didn't say I didn't trust you, Chance, I just hate to impose."

"Katie and I will be fine." He turned and went into the house.

But would she? Joy wondered. Could she live with a man who obviously couldn't stand to be around her?

Chance tried to work on the books, to decide on what stock to move where, but all he could think about was Joy. And why not? She'd been imbedded in his thoughts since the day she'd invaded his life. Now she was in his heart. Dammit! He stood and walked around his bedroom. He couldn't keep living in the same house with her and ignore the fact he wanted her. But something told him that even if he moved out, nothing would stop the unbearable ache.

The baby's soft cry from the other room drew his attention. He hurried down the hall to the nursery and found Katie awake in the crib. "Hi, there, princess."

She made a gurgling sound that tore at his heart. He picked her up and cradled her against his shoulder. He closed his eyes and inhaled her powdery scent as her little hand gripped his shirt. He hadn't held her since they'd returned from the roundup. He'd missed her so much.

"I guess you're hungry," he said. "I better get you changed and see what your mother left for you."

They continued their conversation as he replaced her diaper with a fresh one. He fastened up her pink stretch suit, then carried her downstairs to the kitchen where he found Joy's note with instructions. Taking the bottle from the refrigerator, he heated it in a pan of water on the stove, telling himself he was going to purchase a microwave the next time he was in town.

Warm bottle in hand, he carried Katie upstairs and sat down in the rocker to feed her. She looked a little confused at the new arrangement, but soon began drinking her bottle while Chance reveled in holding her in the crook of his arm.

That was how Joy found them when she returned home. She stood in the doorway as Chance talked softly to her daughter. He was telling Katie all about cows and horses.

"And when you're old enough, princess, I'm going to find the gentlest pony in Texas. Just for you. Then, when you've become an expert rider, you'll be ready for a horse. You'll have the best. Know why? Because I'll train him myself."

Tears filled Joy's eyes as she heard the love in his voice. Was he going to be around? Were they going to be the family Joy had hoped for?

All at once Chance looked toward the door. His smiled faded when he discovered her. "You're home."

She forced a smile. "Yes, didn't have to wait long at the doctor's office."

"Is everything okay?"

His concern surprised her. "Yes, the doctor said I'm in perfect health." *And I can resume sexual relations with my husband,* she added silently. At the thought of Chance making love to her, her body began to warm, and she quickly glanced away.

Chance stood. "I expect you'll want to take over." He gave her Katie. Their hands brushed in the exchange and they nearly bumped heads. He took a step back and slipped his hands in his pockets as if he couldn't stand to touch her.

Joy couldn't take the strain between them any longer. "Chance we need to talk about what happened at the barbecue…"

"Nothing happened, Joy."

"It did, Chance. You kissed me…and I kissed you back."

He cocked an eyebrow. "We were only pretending, just acting like a married couple. I'd say we did a good job of convincing them, don't you? I need to get back to work." He walked out the door before she could stop him. Sadness rushed through her, knowing she wouldn't see him again that day.

Joy carried Katie to the padded table and changed her diaper. Though her heart wasn't in it, she played with her daughter. Then she lifted the baby in her arms and walked to the window. She glanced down at the barn. That's when she saw Chance riding off on his horse. Her heart ached realizing she might have destroyed the best thing that had ever happened to her and Katie.

But was she brave enough to risk everything and go after him?

Chance rode Ace hard, trying to drive Joy from his mind, but it wasn't working. Nothing was working. Not staying away from her, not exhausting himself working from daybreak to dusk. The second he walked into the house, he could smell her. It drove him wild.

Damn. How much more could he take?

He pulled the reins and Ace slowed, then stopped. He patted the horse's lathered coat, then climbed down from the saddle and walked to the row of ancient oaks where a creek wove through the raised tree roots. He led the animal to the water, then crouched down to get a drink himself. Working to slow his own breathing, he removed his hat and wiped the sweat from his brow. He looked out over the valley, wondering if the mustangs would show today. He'd probably frightened them off when he came stampeding in here.

It all had seemed so simple when he'd agreed to Joy's contract. Live at the house for a few years and he would have what he wanted. The ranch. But he hadn't bargained for losing his heart to her and little Katie. He'd brought that baby into the world. How could he not feel something for her? He'd tried to fight it for so long. Whether Joy knew it or not, she needed him, even if she didn't want him.

Hell, he should be used to it. He'd had so much rejection in his past he ought to be tough enough to handle it. Maybe things would have been different if his mother lived. Maybe his dad wouldn't have become a criminal.

And they might still have the family ranch, and their good name. A name that he and his brothers could be proud of. Hell, no wonder Cade and Travis had left town. All these years he'd been fighting off the bad memories. He pulled in a shaky breath. But the pain he felt right now was worse than anything he'd lived through as a kid. And he didn't know if he could do it anymore.

Joy sat with Ella at the kitchen table. She'd driven to the Circle B with the excuse she'd left one of Katie's toys behind. Of course she hadn't, but Joy wanted to see if Chance was there. He wasn't.

Ella poured them some coffee, then glanced to the baby sleeping in her carrier. "Glad you stopped. Haven't seen much of you lately. Chance has been by, but only for a few minutes. He's working too hard."

"I know, but I can't slow him down," Joy said. "He's anxious to get the barn ready for his horses."

"Of course there's more daylight during the summer, but there's a lot more heat, too," Ella warned. "Just make sure that man of yours doesn't overdo. I have to get a little bossy to get Hank to slow down. Course, he's getting up there in years. He'll be sixty-five this August."

"He seems a lot younger," Joy said, remembering how he'd worked the roundup just as hard as any of the younger men.

"I know he's hating this birthday. It means he's a senior citizen. And I doubt I can get him to agree to a party."

"Maybe if you keep it small?"

"Do you think the folks around here would let that happen? Everyone loves Hank."

"What about his family? Does he have any kids?"

Ella shook her head. "His wife, Mae, died about twenty-five years ago. They weren't able to have children."

Joy remembered how Hank had made a fuss over Katie, sad for what he and his wife had missed.

"Hank and Mae had a good life. Never saw two people love each other more. He took her death hard. Didn't know if he'd be able to get past it, either. Then a judge in town asked him if he'd be willing to take in these three brothers. It seemed no one else wanted the troublemakers. Certainly not all three of them at once." Ella grinned. "Hank agreed, and Chance and his brothers arrived at the ranch that weekend. That's when I not only became housekeeper, but nursemaid to those wild Randell boys. Oh it was a rough few months in the beginning. And Chance was the most stubborn. He was so protective of his younger brothers. Wasn't going to let anyone tell them what to do. So Hank made him a deal. If they got in trouble, Chance got punished right along with them."

"Did he?" Joy found she couldn't hear enough about her husband.

"He sure did. If Cade or Travis didn't do their chores, Chance took their punishment. That ended pretty quick when Chance managed to get Cade and Travis to pull their weight, not only here at the ranch, but in school. Hank insisted the boys get good grades and go to college." Something sparkled in the older woman's eyes. "Coming here was the best thing that ever happened to all of them. Oh, Hank would love to have Cade and Travis home."

An idea came to Joy. "Then why can't he? I mean, why can't we call and tell Cade and Travis about the party? Surely with enough warning they can arrange time off for a visit."

Ella blinked in surprise. "You know, it might just work," she said. "I mean, a few months' notice would give them time to make arrangements. And we won't take no for an answer. Besides they haven't met their new sister-in-law."

Joy liked the idea of having a big family around for Katie. "I'd like to meet them, too."

"They'll love Katie...and you." Ella held up her hand. "But, first we have to get them here. So until it's all set, we'll have to keep this a secret."

"I won't tell a soul."

"Not even Chance."

Joy's smiled faded. "No, not even Chance."

Ella studied her for a minute. "Now, tell me the real reason you came by. You and Chance having problems? I know that man can be stubborn, but..."

"No," Joy denied, her voice husky with emotion.

The housekeeper folded her hands over her ample breasts. "And I'm the best cook in the world."

Joy tried but couldn't keep back the tears. "Oh, Ella," she cried and proceeded to tell the housekeeper about their pretend marriage, how Chance wanted the land and she needed a father for Katie to protect her child from in-laws who threatened to take her away.

Ella remained silent as she handed Joy a tissue.

"I'm sorry," Joy said, wiping away tears. "I guess I'm a little overtired."

"So you aren't sleeping?" Ella asked.

She shook her head.

"May I ask where Chance is sleeping?"

Heat rushed to Joy's face. "Down the hall in another bedroom," she whispered.

Ella sighed. "That explains a lot. I bet you two sharing a room here during the roundup was interesting. No wonder Chance was in a foul mood in the mornings." She chuckled, then quickly sobered. "It's probably for the best...for now."

"It is?"

"Honey, you just had a baby not long ago. Give yourself some time. Men are in too much of an all-fired hurry anyway. Serves him right to have to wait awhile. *You* make the decision about the sleeping arrangements. After all, he agreed to this."

Joy had thought that was what she'd wanted, a business relationship, but she wasn't so sure any more. "I've tried to talk to him, but he avoids me."

"That's because his feelings have changed. The man looks at you like he could eat you up."

Excitement raced through Joy. "He does?"

"Yes, he does. I saw it from the first time you were together. That's the reason I wasn't too surprised when you two married so soon." Ella grew serious. "Just don't toy with him, Joy. Chance is a good man, he deserves a woman who will love him. Make sure you want *him,* and not what he can do for you."

That evening, Joy fixed one of Chance's favorite dishes, lasagna. When he walked into the kitchen she was both relieved and nervous. Of course, as much as she tried, she couldn't find the courage to talk about what was going on between them. And his stony look didn't help the situation.

"Is the lasagna okay?" she finally asked, trying to keep the trembling out of her voice.

"It's good."

Joy's tasted like cardboard. "I was surprised today to see how much you've done in the barn. I didn't know the work would be so extensive."

He stopped eating. "If there's something you don't approve of, tell me."

"I didn't say I didn't approve." She drew a breath to calm herself. "I went to the Circle B today and had a nice visit with Ella. She told me stories about you and your brothers."

His steely-gray eyes darted to hers, his anger evident. "You want to know anything about me—ask me."

"Chance, I didn't snoop into your past, Ella just

told me some cute stories.'' Her own anger began to build. ''Look, I'm just trying to carry on a civilized conversation with you, but it doesn't look like that's going to happen.'' She got up from the table and rushed out of the room.

No, she wasn't going to cry, she told herself as she climbed the stairs and walked down the hall to her bedroom. She checked on Katie, then collapsed on her bed. How could she get through to the man? How could she convince him her feelings for him had changed? That she wanted him to be her husband. A shiver raced through her body at the realization. Exhausted, she closed her eyes and let sleep take over.

The sound of a loud crash jerked Joy awake. She gasped and tried to focus on something, but the room was pitch-black, and she was still in her jeans and T-shirt. There was a flash of light, and another loud clap of thunder. It was storming. The sound of rain against the window quickly intensified. She got up, brushing the hair away from her face, remembering the scene at supper and her quick departure.

The wind picked up as the rain turned into a downpour that was coming though the open window. Joy turned on the light and hurried to close it. The stubborn sash refused to budge. She had to do something quickly or her room would be flooded. Her clothes were already getting drenched.

A lightning bolt flashed across the angry sky, and suddenly the lights went out. All at once the sash broke and the pane came crashing down, breaking glass all over her. Joy screamed.

Everything happened so fast. Katie began to cry just as Chance burst into the room.

"Joy, what happened?"

"Stop!" she cried. "There's broken glass on the floor."

Chance swore. "Are you hurt?"

"No, I have shoes on, but glass shattered all over me. Please go and see if Katie's all right. She's scared."

"Okay, but don't move, honey," he ordered. "I'll be right back."

Joy listened as Chance soothed Katie with his calming voice. The worst of the storm had moved on, but the rain was still coming down heavily. Shivering and wet, Joy stepped away from the window, not knowing how much glass she had on her. She didn't think she'd been cut.

A few minutes later, Chance came in carrying a flashlight and wearing boots. He directed the light on the window and swore, then ran it over Joy.

"Were you cut?" he asked as he helped her out of the pile of broken glass and rain.

"I'm not sure," she said, not able to keep the tremble out of her voice. "I think there's some pieces of glass in my clothes."

He scanned the light over her. "There are, I can see them. You also have some small cuts on the back of your hand."

"What do I do?"

"First, we'll have to get you out of your clothes. Do you have any scissors?"

"Bathroom."

"Come on, let's go."

They made their way down the hall. Once inside, he set the flashlight on the counter facing toward the ceiling. "Where are they?"

"Top drawer."

He brought out the small scissors. "I think the safest way is to get into the shower. Any tiny shards of glass will wash down the drain."

She stepped into the deep bathtub, tennis shoes and all. Surprisingly he followed her. "What are you doing?"

"I'm going to help you get out of those clothes."

She hadn't realized she'd been shivering until she tried to talk. "I can get undressed."

"I need to cut your T-shirt off, I don't want you pulling it over your head, just in case of small splinters."

She was so cold all she could do was nod. He quickly went to work on cutting away her shirt, leaving her in her bra. He then used the scissors on her jeans. That took a while longer. Finally she was standing there in only her nursing bra and panties and a pair of soggy tennis shoes.

He turned on the water. Joy gasped at the cold and jumped into his arms.

"Ssh, babe, it'll warm up in a minute." He was getting drenched, too. Ignoring his soaked jeans and boots, Chance made sure her entire body was rinsed clean of any glass.

His gentleness brought tears to her eyes. He was concerned about her. She wanted to hold on to him forever, but the sound of her daughter's frantic crying brought her back to reality. She could feel her milk coming in. "I need to feed Katie."

"You finish washing, and I'll get your robe." He stepped out and returned with her terry robe and two towels. Thankfully, he left her alone to dry off. By the time she came out of the bathroom, he was there holding a sobbing Katie.

"Guess she wants her mother." He handed the baby over. "The nursery is safe, just stay out of your bedroom. I'll get some plastic from the porch."

"Okay," she said, and followed the glowing flashlight on the table next to the rocker. She sat down, opened her robe and her hungry daughter began to nurse. "It's okay, sweetie. Mama's here."

Joy shut her eyes, wondering what would have happened tonight if Chance hadn't been here. Terror raced through her, not wanting to think about it.

Outside, all that was left of the storm was a low rumbling. She heard Chance in her bedroom, covering the window.

When he walked into the nursery, Joy didn't cover herself. The man had seen her at her worst, during childbirth, looking like a drowned rat in a bathtub.

"I'm going to move you and Katie into my room."

"But…"

"Don't worry, I'll sleep downstairs on the sofa."

"I wasn't worried," she said. "I just didn't want to put you out."

"You're not. I doubt I'll be sleeping much anyway. I'll repair the window in the morning. But for now, stay out of your room. There's glass everywhere." He picked up the portable crib in the corner and carried it down the hall.

Joy rubbed her daughter's head. "We're very lucky to have Chance around." Katie stopped nursing and made a cooing sound.

"I feel the same way." Joy looked toward the doorway. "I only hope I can find a way to convince him."

* * *

Chance couldn't stop shaking. He hadn't been able to since he'd heard Joy's screams. He'd thought something had happened to her. He couldn't stand that. When she'd nearly jumped into his arms in the shower, he didn't think he would ever let her go.

He managed to set up the crib, then went to the bed and smoothed out the crumpled sheets. He didn't want Joy to see how he'd used the bed as a torture chamber. He hadn't been able to sleep in here since he'd moved in. Not with her down the hall. He lay awake every night, aching for her. Aching for what he could never have.

"Chance." Joy's soft voice interrupted his thoughts.

He went to the door, and she walked in carrying a sleeping Katie. "The crib is ready."

"Good." She went to the corner and laid her daughter down. Chance watched as her hand lingered over the child, stroking gently. He closed his eyes and thought about Joy's hands on him.

Joy began to unwind the towel from her head, then he watched as she tried to comb her fingers through the tangled strands. "It's wet, but I can braid it for now," she said.

He saw her hands shake and went to help. He knew he was asking for more trouble as he turned her around and took over.

"I'm not much good at this." He took a slow even breath. Awkwardly, he separated the wavy strands, then worked them into a single braid, but not before he inhaled her soft scent that was pure Joy. He used a piece of rawhide he had on the dresser and tied the end.

"All done." He had to get some distance between them. He started out of the room, but she was close on his heels. The sooner he got away from her the better.

"Please don't leave me, Chance," she whispered. There was trembling in her voice as she stood in the doorway.

He stopped in the hall, but didn't look at her. If he did he was a goner for sure.

"Chance...don't go," she said again.

He fought the excitement racing through him. She was just scared, he told himself. "I have to, Joy."

"No you don't, I want you to stay with me. I'm frightened, but not because of what happened tonight. I'm afraid you'll leave me for good."

He turned around. "I'm not going anywhere unless you want me to."

"But you're so angry with me." She blinked and he could hear the tears in her voice. "Oh, Chance, I...I didn't want to push you away before...I got scared," she admitted. "Scared about what I was starting to feel for you."

In a second, he closed the distance between them and pulled her into his arms. "Sshh, Joy. It's okay."

"No, it's not." She drew back. "I never want you to think I didn't want you. I do...as my husband."

The air was trapped in Chance's lungs. "I am your husband."

She shook her head. "I want a *real* husband."

His pulse was pounding so loudly in his ears, he thought it would wake the baby. "You don't know what you're saying..."

She nodded slowly. "I do. I want you to make love to me, Chance."

His hands shook as he cupped her face. "Oh, Joy. Do you mean it?" he breathed. "It will change everything."

She raised up on her toes and placed a kiss on his mouth. "I hope so. Please, Chance, say you want me, too."

"Oh, babe, you have no idea." His mouth closed over hers in a hungry kiss, promising her they would spend the night as close to heaven as they would get on this earth.

Chapter Ten

If this was a dream he didn't want to wake up.

Chance swung Joy up into his arms and carried her across the room to the bed. He laid her down on the mattress and started to pull away, but her arms were locked tight around his neck, refusing to let him go.

"Don't leave me," she said, her voice husky soft.

Chance's pulse raced, seeing the uncertainty on her face, wanting to reassure her. "Oh, babe, nothing short of a stampede could drive me away," he promised. "It's just, these wet jeans are mighty uncomfortable."

She finally released him. Never taking his eyes off her, Chance stood back in the dim light, toed off his boots and kicked them aside. His hands were trembling like an awkward teenager's when he worked the button and zipper on his pants. Not an easy task with her eyes on him, heating his body to near boiling.

Somehow he managed to strip off his jeans, then tossed them in the corner, leaving him in a pair of damp briefs.

"Oh, you are a beautiful man, Chance Randell," she whispered, her voice heavy with desire.

Pleased that she liked what she saw, but aware that his body had more than its share of scars, Chance smiled. "Thank you, ma'am, but I'm just a battered and bruised cowboy."

He came back to the bed and leaned over her. Now it was his turn. Working loose the belt on her robe, he tugged it open, then pushed aside the material that hid her from view. His hungry gaze roamed over her breasts, full and ripe, the rosy nipples puckered to the perfect buds, just begging to be touched. He lingered over her stomach, and a waist he could span with his hands. His breathing nearly stopped when he moved on to her shapely thighs and long smooth legs. The past weeks he could only imagine what she looked like. She was a hundred times better than his dreams.

"Oh, Joy. You're the one who's beautiful."

Her hands fluttered over her stomach. "I have marks from my pregnancy."

He brushed them away. "Nothing can take away from your beauty." His shaky hand traced over her stomach, then upward to her breast. She gasped, and he pulled away. "Did I hurt you?"

"No. I want you to touch me." She took his wrist and guided his hand back. "Don't stop."

Chance didn't want to stop and wasn't sure he could. He had wanted Joy for weeks, almost from the moment she'd appeared in his life. And as long as she stayed, he wanted to sample paradise.

He lay down beside her and pulled her into an embrace as their mouths met. One kiss turned into another, each one more and more demanding. He drove his tongue inside, tasting her secrets, wanting and needing everything she was willing to give him.

His mouth left hers and trailed kisses along her jaw, down her neck to her breast. Cupping the plump flesh in his hand, he drew the hard bud into his mouth and listened to her soft moans of pleasure.

Joy raked her fingers into Chance's hair and held him. The sweet torture was driving her crazy. She pressed her body against his, telling him she wanted more. As if he knew her every desire, his hands moved over her, smoothing his fingers up and down her back, cupping her bottom and pressing her tight against him.

Chance tore his mouth away and drew back far enough to look at her. She watched him struggle for a breath, his eyes intense with longing. He braced the sides of her face with his hands. "I want to make love to you, Joy."

"I want that, too." She pressed her body into his hardness and listened to his groan.

"I don't have any protection. I mean...I didn't know this would happen. I didn't even know if you were able to..."

Joy put her finger to his lips. He drew it inside his mouth and sucked gently. She gasped. "The doctor said I was fine. In fact, she gave me some contraceptives. Condoms."

"Where?"

"In the bathroom, top drawer behind my makeup."

Chance gave her a quick kiss and was out of the bed. He grabbed the flashlight, hurried into the bathroom and opened the drawer. Finding the foil-wrapped treasures, he returned to the bedroom. He tossed them on the table, then stripped off his briefs. After readying himself, he slipped back into bed.

"I want this to be good for you," he said, unable to hold back the strain in his voice. He tried to take a calming breath, but it didn't work. "I mean, I don't want to hurt you."

Her hands cupped his face. "You can only hurt me if you leave."

He smiled. "I don't see much chance of that any time soon."

When he kissed her, her body raised up, relaying her need. She tore her mouth from his, her gaze dark and searching. "Please, Chance, make love to me."

He didn't need to be asked again and shifted over her. His tongue dove deep into her mouth as his hand moved between them. He groaned when he found her ready. Parting her legs, he raised himself over her and slowly pushed inside. With a breathy whimper, Joy molded her body to his. He paused, waiting for her to adjust, and for himself to regain control. Sweat broke out on his face as he worked to keep his movement slow and easy, but she would have none of it. Her soft moans and encouraging whispers drove him to increase their pace.

With each stroke her breath became more ragged, and her face glowed as they moved together as one. Suddenly, her eyes grew large with wonder, and she whispered his name. Then she buried her face against his chest to muffle her cries of release. At that same moment, Chance threw back his head and growled, and his body shuddered as he found his way to heaven, too.

Seconds later, or was it minutes? Chance wasn't sure, he rolled over and pulled Joy tight against him. Silently, he held her close, not wanting to break the spell. His emotions were too raw, and he couldn't deal

with them. No woman had ever made him feel the
things Joy had made him feel. And it frightened him.

Joy made a purring sound and moved closer to him,
her arms draping over his chest. "You okay?" she
asked.

"I thought I was the one who was supposed to ask
that."

"But you aren't talking." She moved her bare foot
along his calf.

"And if you keep that up, we'll be doing more than
talking."

She raised her head and smiled. "Really? You want
me again?"

In a New York minute, he thought. "Fishing for
compliments?" He kissed her nose.

"Just wanted to know if you were...pleased."

His heart pounded as he heard the doubt in her
voice. "I'm not very good with words, Joy. But,
damn, woman, you've had me half crazy ever since
the morning you woke up in my arms."

"So you're not angry with me anymore?" Her hand
caressed his chest and he lost it.

"No, I'm not angry. In fact I've never felt better in
my life." He cupped her face and leaned down to kiss
her, relaying to her just how happy she'd made him.

Joy blinked and finally opened her eyes to discover
sunlight shining through the window. Her brain focused on where she was. Chance's bed. What time was
it? She rolled over and looked at the bedside clock.
Seven o'clock. Katie. She sat up and the blanket
dropped, exposing her nakedness. Oh, Lord. She
quickly covered herself, recalling last night's events.
Chance had made love to her. Twice.

Joy glanced at the empty side of the bed. He was gone. Panic hit her as she climbed out of bed, gathered up her discarded robe from the floor and slipped it on. Had he regretted what happened last night? Her cheeks reddened, recalling what taken place between them. Never in her life had she experienced anything like what she'd shared with Chance. Not even with Blake. Chance made her feel so much…. She shut her eyes as the emotions hit her all at once. By giving herself to Chance last night, she had closed that chapter of her life…her life as Mrs. Blake Spencer.

The sound of Chance's voice snapped Joy back to reality. She quickly wiped away her tears and put on a smile, but not fast enough. Chance appeared in the room with Katie in his arms. He had on a fresh pair of jeans and nothing else.

He gave Joy a puzzled look. "Morning," he said, eyeing her tears. His smile faded. "Princess and I got up earlier and thought we'd let you sleep a while, but she's getting impatient for breakfast. Is something wrong?"

"No," she said a little too quickly.

He handed her Katie, and immediately her daughter began searching for her food. Joy looked up at Chance and wondered why she suddenly felt awkward. He'd seen her naked, touched and kissed every part of her. Joy's body grew warm, and she had to glance away as she opened the lapel on her robe and guided her daughter to her breast.

"I guess things are a little awkward the morning after," Chance said.

Joy tried to speak, but he held up his hand and stopped her.

"Let's not make excuses, okay?" He grabbed a

shirt from the closet and picked up a pair of boots. "Let's just chalk last night up as two people in need." Before she could stop him he'd walked out.

What was wrong with her? She had made love to this man, why couldn't she tell him how she felt about him? But she knew her own insecurities kept her from going after him. She didn't have any assurance Chance would stay around. Would their marriage be a real one? Only one thing Joy knew—last night Chance had made such sweet love to her. And there was no doubt, she was head over heels in love with him.

Joy looked down at her daughter, who suckled contentedly at her breast. "How are we going to let him know that we love him, Katie?"

The tiny girl's eyes rounded as if she understood. One thing Joy knew for sure, she wasn't going to let Chance sulk for two weeks. She planned on making sure he knew how she felt today.

Chance had wasted the entire morning. He hadn't done that in years. He'd driven into town to get someone to replace the broken bedroom window. Then he'd ordered feed to be delivered the next day. He even went shopping for clothes. Anything to keep from going back to the house so Joy could tell him that she'd made a mistake.

Now, he had no choice. He had to face her. Hank had always taught him to deal with his problems head-on. Chance drove his truck up the gravel drive and parked by the back porch. He could agree that last night had happened too soon. Too soon for Joy to know what she wanted. She had buried a husband not even a year ago. But how could he go back to the way things were before? He didn't want a business relationship. Damn. He couldn't handle that. He already ached for Joy, all of her, and he wouldn't settle for anything less. A real marriage, with her in his bed every night.

Determined, he climbed out of the car and reached in the back for his purchases. Heading for the steps, he stopped to pet the dogs, then went inside. He drew a breath when he heard Joy in the kitchen. He walked into the room, finding her busy at the stove. She was dressed in leggings and a white blouse that nearly covered her cute bottom. He quickly curbed his sensual thoughts. On the table Katie was sitting in her carrier chattering away and waving her arms. Everything he'd ever wanted was right here. Did he dare to reach out for it?

Joy turned and gasped when she saw Chance standing at the door. Warmth surged through her as her gaze combed over the tall cowboy dressed in jeans and the shirt he'd pulled from the closet this morning. His hat was tipped back from his face, showing her his best stony look.

"So, you decided to come home," she said, then turned her back on him. She wasn't going to rush into his arms. Not until he let her know where he'd been for the last six hours.

"I needed to get some things done. Did they come out and replace the window?"

"Yes, all done," Joy said as she continued to stir the sauce on the stove. "Three hours ago. And the electricity came on, too." She couldn't take any more and swung around. "Where were you, Chance?"

He shrugged. "Rode into town."

She placed her hands on her hips. "Town. That's all, you were in town? You didn't think that I'd be worried? Well, mister, you better think again, because I nearly called the sheriff. How dare you leave without…?'' She stopped, but her tears didn't. ''Oh, what's the use?'' She started to leave, but Chance hurried after her. When he took her arm, she fought him, but his strength won out and he held her captive against his chest.

''I'm sorry, Joy,'' he said. ''I had no idea you'd worry about me. I mean, I was just trying to burn off some anger.''

''Why?'' She looked up at him, seeing his stubborn set jaw. ''What did I do this morning that made you angry?''

''I couldn't take seeing your regrets. You wanting your husband.''

''You think I regretted last night?'' She stood back. ''I admit that I was a little confused. I was married to Blake a long time. I loved him. When you walked in I was…was saying good-bye.'' Her eyes met his questioning silver gaze. ''I realized I needed to move on. Chance, last night I wasn't thinking about Blake.'' Her voice grew husky. ''I was thinking of you. There were no regrets.''

Chance's pulse drummed in his ears, but he heard every precious word she spoke. ''You better mean it, because I can't go back to the way things were.''

Joy shook her head. ''I don't want to, either.''

He squeezed his eyes shut, his emotions swelling in his chest. He drew her into his arms, unable to stand the separation a second longer. His mouth came down on hers in a kiss that told her of his need and hunger. By the time he released her, they were both breathing hard.

''I'm sorry about earlier….'' he said.

Joy kissed him again to stop his words. "I guess I have to work at convincing you that it's you I want," she breathed against his mouth.

"I wouldn't mind at all, ma'am."

Joy went to the table and saw that Katie had fallen asleep. "I better put her down for a nap." She looked up at Chance. "That will leave me with some free time on my hands."

Chance picked up the carrier and placed an arm around Joy. Together, they made their way to the stairs. "I can think of several things to keep your hands busy."

"Don't get dressed yet," Chance said. "I brought you something." Wearing only his jeans, he quickly disappeared from the bedroom, leaving Joy in her robe and with a smile on her face.

They'd spent the last hour in bed, making love. They hadn't talked much about their new relationship, but Joy knew that Chance would never leave her or Katie. He might not have spoken the words, but she knew he cared for her.

He returned to the room with several bags. Joy's excitement grew. "What did you buy?"

"Something that every cowgirl needs." He pulled out a large box and opened it, revealing a pair of buckskin boots.

"Oh, Chance. They're beautiful." Her gaze met his. "But how did you know my size?"

"Looked inside a pair of your shoes. And guessed some, but if they don't fit, you can exchange them." He pulled out a pair of socks from the bag and handed them to her. "Try 'em on."

Katie's cry came from the next room.

"I'll get her," Chance said.

Joy didn't waste any time pulling on the socks, then worked her feet into the beautifully tooled boots. She stood up and sighed, feeling the soft leather caress her feet. They felt so good. She walked to the door as Chance came in carrying Katie.

"You look great, but you need something else to complete the outfit. Look in the other bags."

Joy frowned, but she loved that he'd bought her gifts. "Chance, what have you done?" She opened another package and found two new pairs of boot-cut jeans. "Oh, Chance. You didn't need to do this."

Balancing the baby, he leaned forward and kissed her. "I wanted to."

"But..."

"Just open the other bags and see what I got for Katie."

"You shopped at a baby store?"

He nodded. "I thought since she's been growing so much, she needed some new things, too. I didn't want her jealous of her mother."

Joy opened a box from a children's store and had to blink back tears. Inside was a pink stretch suit that had Daddy's Little Cowgirl embroidered on the front. "Oh, this is so cute."

He looked a little embarrassed. "It's not too much?"

"No, it's adorable. I can't wait to see her in it."

"Well, how about tonight? We could go out to dinner," he said. "I know you've been cooking, but we've never gone out."

He looked so sweet. "You mean, like a date?" she asked.

He cocked an eyebrow. "I thought we could just go to a local restaurant—with Katie of course."

"Oh, Chance. Katie and I would love to."

He grinned, and she felt her chest tighten. How she loved this man.

"You can wear your new jeans and boots," he said.

Joy couldn't stand it any longer. She raised up on her boot-covered toes and kissed him sweetly. "Thank you."

"You're welcome." His eyes darkened as his head lowered to hers, and he returned her kiss with a little more heat. He growled. "I can't get enough of you. So you better get ready, or I'll forget about our date." He pushed her away. "I'll take care of the princess."

Joy gathered her things and headed for the shower. In ten minutes she was finished. She slipped on her soft, prewashed jeans then her boots. They felt a little awkward at first as she learned to walk in them. She added a white blouse and a new belt that Chance had also bought her. Fluffing her hair around her shoulders, she stepped out of the bathroom.

Chance was waiting. He, too, had changed into clean jeans and a starched sky-blue western-cut shirt. He was holding Katie in her new outfit. What a picture they made.

"You ready to go eat, Mrs. Randell?"

All she could do was nod, praying that this wasn't a dream. That they could be a real family.

Fifteen minutes later, they arrived at the outskirts of San Angelo and pulled into the parking lot of Sally's Kitchen. The second they walked in the door, Chance was greeted by nearly everyone, from waitresses to patrons. After introductions, Chance directed her to a booth and they sat down. Soon people appeared at their table, anxious for a peek at Katie and to toss a few teasing remarks to Chance about not being around lately.

Finally a blond waitress in her mid-forties cleared everyone away. "Hi, I'm Sally Roberts, owner of this fine establishment." She smiled and shook Joy's hand. "So, how'd you manage to lasso this good-looking wrangler?"

Joy blushed as she looked at the man across from her. "I just got lucky. I was in the right place at the right time." She'd never forget Chance coming to her rescue when she was in labor.

Sally mumbled something about how she'd like to find that place, then pulled her pad from her pocket and took their order.

After she left, Chance leaned across the table. "I'm sorry. I had no idea that we would cause such a ruckus."

"I don't mind. Katie loves the attention. In fact, I was thinking that maybe we should invite a few people to the house. Everyone was so nice during the roundup."

"It's a good idea. But don't make extra work for yourself. You're busy enough with Katie."

"I'd love it. I want your friends and neighbors coming to our home."

"Why don't we start small with Hank and Ella?" he suggested. "I was going to have Hank help me transfer some of the horses I'm training to the ranch. That is, if it's okay with you."

Joy was touched that he wanted to discuss his plans with her. "Oh, I can't wait. It means you'll be working at home. You'll be around more."

He gave her a lopsided grin. "So, you like me around?"

Joy felt the heat rush to her face. She wasn't going to hide her feelings from him. They were both still a little insecure about this new relationship, but she wanted to help change that. She crooked her finger for him to lean over the table. When he did, she cupped the back of his neck and planted a kiss on him that stirred them both. She finally released him after hearing several murmurs from the crowd. "Does that answer your question?"

"All I can say is you better eat your supper fast," he said, his voice low enough so that she was the only one who heard. "I need to get you home."

Chance couldn't drive any faster, not with his precious cargo aboard. But his thoughts kept wandering to his wife and how much he wanted her. Finally the ranch was in view. He pulled up the drive and helped Joy and Katie into the house. Katie was nearly asleep, but Joy was going to try and nurse her so she wouldn't wake up during the night.

Upstairs in the nursery, Joy sat in the rocker and began to chat with her daughter. Chance loved to watch them together, but thought he should give them some privacy. He turned to leave.

"Chance, don't go," Joy said.

His heart swelled as he came to her side and knelt down. He caressed Katie's head. "You two look so beautiful together. I could watch you forever." He had trouble keeping the emotion out of his voice.

"I love this time with Katie." She touched his face. "I don't want to shut you out, Chance. This morning

I was confused over everything I was feeling. It was all just so new…a little scary.''

"How are you now?''

She glanced down at her daughter. "I want you in our lives. We need you.''

A rush went through Chance as if he'd ridden out the eight-second buzzer and won the grand prize. Nothing in his life had ever been this perfect. And he wasn't about to question it anymore. If fate had given him Joy and Katie, who was he to argue?

The next morning, Chance finished with the feed delivery and headed up to the house to see his girls. He ambled along the walkway and smiled at the antics of the puppies playing in the yard. Not too far in the future he would need to fence off a section for Katie, maybe build her a swing. He glanced at the row of colorful flowers along the porch, realizing how much things had changed in the last few weeks. He smiled at the pansies, knowing he'd changed, too. Who would have thought he'd be so happy living with a houseful of females? And loving it so much.

He stepped into the kitchen to find Joy at the table chopping vegetables for soup. He placed his hat on the hook and went straight to his wife. Pulling her into his arms, he kissed her thoroughly.

"Well, Mr. Randell, that was a nice greeting.''

"Not as nice as the one this morning,'' he teased, remembering he hadn't gotten out of bed until well after six. "Of course, when we get livestock I can't be as lazy.''

Joy's blue eyes sparkled with mischief. "I guess we'll have to wake up earlier, then.''

Chance groaned and was bending to kiss her again when he heard the front doorbell.

"Who could that be?" Joy asked.

"I'll go and check." Chance walked through the dining room to the entry and pulled open the door. A well-dressed couple in their sixties stood on the porch. The man wore a dark business suit and the woman, a tailored pink dress. They definitely weren't from around here. Suddenly a feeling of dread rushed through him. They had to be the Spencers. He'd bet his life on it.

"I want to see Joy Spencer," the gray-haired man said. "And don't try and tell me she doesn't live here. I know better."

Chance planted his feet apart and blocked the entrance. "I don't care what you know..." he glared at the man who had made Joy's life miserable, "...you're not coming here and making demands. I don't know who the hell you are." He started to shut the door.

The woman stepped to the threshold and said, "We're the Spencers. I'm Margaret, and this is my husband, James. Joy was married to our son. I'm afraid there was a misunderstanding and she ran off without a word. We're worried about the baby. Our grandchild. Can you tell us if Joy and the child are okay?"

"The only misunderstanding was that the woman kidnapped my grandchild," James Spencer interrupted.

"Joy has the right to take her child anywhere she wants," Chance said. "She's the mother. And if you don't leave now, I'm calling the sheriff."

The woman looked at him pleadingly. "Please, Joy

and I used to be friends. May I talk to her? I know we can straighten this out.''

Chance studied the handsome woman with the ash-blond hair, and perfectly manicured nails. "She's fine," Chance offered. "But now is not a good time."

"I'm not going anywhere," Jim Spencer said. "Not until I see my grandchild. I have rights."

Chance was angry now. He stood face-to-face with Spencer. "Not in this house, you don't."

Spencer looked him over. "You must be that Randell guy she hooked up with. The investigator dug up a long list on you," he said with a sneer. "Damn, she couldn't even wait until Blake was cold in the grave before she took up with another man."

"James!" Margaret gasped, then glared at her husband. "You promised me. I only agreed to come if you were civil."

"Well, I'm not going to stand here and let this ranch hand tell me what I can do. I mean to get custody of that baby."

"No you won't."

All three turned to see Joy come into the entry.

"Joy, you're all right," Margaret cried. Chance was surprised to see the concern in the woman's eyes. "And the baby? How could you run away from us…so soon after we lost Blake?"

Joy stood next to Chance. "Because you were going to allow your husband to take my baby from me. How did you find me?"

"Birth records," James said. "But why did you come to this godforsaken place?" he said, looking around the old house. "I won't allow you to raise my grandchild here."

"Well, Jim, it looks like you don't have a choice," Joy said.

James Spencer sneered. "Then you don't know me very well. You may have stolen my son away, but I'm not going to let you have my only heir. And if you think I'd let you and this son of an ex-con get his hands on her, you'd better think again."

Chance flinched as if the man had struck him, but he masked any reaction.

"And you, Randell, your record isn't so clean, either. Like father, like son, I'd say."

Chance felt Joy tense as Spencer spewed out the words. "Just get out," she cried. "Get off my property."

"We're leaving...for now. But we're staying at the Riverwalk Inn in town...until tomorrow." Spencer pulled a card from his pocket. "Also here's my lawyer's number. You'd better get yourself one, because you're going to need him." With those words, James Spencer turned and headed down the steps to the rental parked in the circular drive.

Margaret hesitated, giving Joy a pleading look. "Joy, you shouldn't have left. I could have helped you." She followed her husband.

Chance closed the door as the car drove away. "I'm sorry, I was trying to get rid of them."

Joy started to shake. She clasped her hands together, telling herself she had to be strong. She couldn't give in to the fear. She'd known this day would come. She turned to Chance for reassurance.

"I'm sorry, Joy," he said. "I'm sorry about all this."

"Why? It's not your fault," she said, wondering why he suddenly was so distant.

"But it is. I knew my past would someday end up hurting you and Katie."

"What are you talking about?"

"Spencer came after you because he's got ammunition. You know my daddy went to prison. He doesn't want me raising his granddaughter. And I don't blame him."

"Chance, James was just trying to scare us. We've got to stick together…as a family…and fight him. Besides what your father did in the past and what you did as a juvenile has nothing to do with the man you are today."

"People around here have long memories, Joy. Some still resent the Randells. And why not, my daddy rustled their cattle. I'm surprised they didn't hang him from the nearest tree. Don't you see, I don't want my connection to you and Katie to cause you to lose her." His chest constricted. "I can't let that happen." He swallowed the lump in his throat, knowing he was about to lose everything, but he had no choice. "Dammit, I care about you both too much for that. And the best thing for me to do is leave."

She searched his face. "What are you saying, Chance?"

"You and Katie are better off if I get out of your lives altogether. I'll come back later and get my things."

The hardest thing he'd ever had to do was turn away from her and walk through the house, knowing he'd never be able to erase the hurt he saw on Joy's face.

And he'd never be able to ease the pain in his heart.

Chapter Eleven

Four hours later, Chance was exhausted. He'd been repairing a section of fence in the north pasture. The overworked muscles in his arms twitched as he tugged the barbed wire tight around the post.

But he had to keep going. He had to do something to erase the memory of Joy from his mind, to stop thinking about what he'd almost had. Not the land. He didn't give a damn about the land. It was Joy and Katie he wanted. But, now, he had lost them both.

Damn, he'd been so afraid for Joy. He knew all about powerful men and what they could do. James Spencer could make him look like scum. If there was the slightest chance that Joy could lose Katie…he'd never forgive himself. He had to walk away.

Sweat trickled down his face when he jerked the wire taut. He was about to secure it with a horseshoe nail when suddenly the metal cord sprang loose. He jumped back, but not in time. The wire whiplashed along his body, his arm catching the worst blow.

"Damn you, Rufus. You're more trouble than you're worth." Chance eyed his shirt. The sleeve was shredded and streaked with blood from the stinging wound underneath.

Still cursing the Circle B's resident bull who'd torn down the fence to get to the herd of heifers, Chance marched back to the truck and opened the first-aid kit.

The antiseptic stung, but he welcomed the painful distraction. He needed something to block the pain he felt inside. It had only been a few hours since he'd left the house and Joy, and he'd been doing everything to keep from running back to what he knew now he could never have.

He rolled his sleeve down and started toward the fence when he saw a rider coming over the rise. Squinting into the sun, Chance recognized Hank on his chestnut gelding, Buddy. At the sight of the rancher riding way out here, Chance couldn't help but wonder if something was wrong.

When Hank reached Chance, he quickly climbed down. His horse wandered over to the shade and the water trough.

Chance didn't hide his panic. "What's happened?"

Hank took a moment to slow his breathing as he removed his hat and wiped the sweat from his forehead. "Maybe you better tell me. I just got off the phone with your wife. She said you left her."

The words made him sound like a jerk, but he guessed that's what he was. "It's for the best." He walked back to the fence, not wanting to discuss it.

Hank followed him. "It's for the best to leave your wife and child? Do you know how lucky you were to find a gal like Joy?" Each word was like a stab in Chance's heart.

"And what about Katie?" Hank continued. "How can you walk away from her?" The older man shook his head. "Doesn't seem right."

"We Randells don't always do the right thing."

Hank glared at him. "You know I never once ever took a hand to you or your brothers. But right now, I'm itchin' to knock you down a peg or two." He released a tired breath. "Talk to me, son. Let me help you."

Chance looked Hank in the eye, expecting to see disappointment, but not finding it. As always, there was only compassion.

"Do you love her?" the older man asked.

Chance turned away and picked up the barbed wire. "That's not the point. It was best for everyone that I left. The judge will see it that way, too."

"I don't understand. I thought the reason you married Joy was to help her keep Katie."

"Her in-laws are loaded. Spencer threatened to drag out my past...and Jack's. You know there are people around here that still haven't forgotten what happened."

Hank groaned. "And you're tops on that list. Chance, when are you going to stop doing penance for your daddy's sins? Jack was the one who stole the cattle. Not you. Not Cade or Travis." Hank placed his hands on his hips. "Yeah, there are people around here who will never forget what he did. There are also people who know and respect you, Chance. Who know the honest man you are. A good man who's a hard-working rancher and who breeds and trains the best saddle horses around. And for the last twenty years, a man that I've been honored to think of as my son."

Chance couldn't speak for the lump in his throat.

Hank had no trouble. "And if you're the man I always thought you were, you wouldn't let some hot-shot from the city scare you away. In fact, you'd be in that truck and headed back to your wife. Back to a woman who needs you to help fight off those damn Spencers. Chance, you have to know how much Joy loves you."

Chance had never heard sweeter words. His pulse pounded with excitement. "Did she tell you that?"

"Do you think she would have called and asked me to find you and bring you home if she didn't?"

Hope surged through him, but there were doubts. "But what if I'm not good enough?"

"Only in your eyes." Hank sighed. "Remember the juvenile judge that you appeared in front of when you were about fourteen?"

After twenty years, Chance couldn't forget the man. "Judge Hayhurst. He almost took me away from you. Said I wasn't worth the effort."

"But he didn't take you away, because I fought to keep you and your brothers." Hank smiled. "I ran into him a couple of months ago. He asked about you. Said he'd been hearing good things about you and your horses. He also said he wanted to bring his grand-daughter to pick out one. Now, I'd say that makes you pretty trustworthy."

Hank retrieved his horse and climbed on. "You just have to convince yourself." He rode off.

Chance watched the rider disappear over the rise, wishing he could call him back. For the first time in a long time, he didn't want to be alone. He sat on the tailgate, and his thoughts turned to Joy, to the first time he ever saw her. Her trust had been unwavering as he delivered her baby. All she had to do was flash those blue eyes at him, and he felt like the king of the world. He'd never wanted to risk his heart, but Joy and Katie came along and stole it before he knew what happened. He knew he'd give his life for his family.

Emotions clogged his throat as he realized he was a good man. He wasn't a shiftless thief like his daddy. He'd worked hard to make a good living. He could turn the Kirby Ranch into a profitable business they all could be proud of. With Joy's love he could do anything. And he could be a good husband and father. All he had to do was prove it.

He stood, then flipped up the tailgate and hurried to the cab. Starting the truck, he hit the gas and raced along the dirt road. First he had to see Spencer and let him know he couldn't come to Texas and threaten a Randell and his family. Then if it wasn't too late, he'd go to Joy and tell her how much she meant to him. How much he wanted a real marriage.

Chance stopped by the Circle B just long enough to clean up and change clothes before he drove into San Angelo. He parked at one of the large chain hotels along the riverwalk, then stopped by the front desk to let the Spencers know he wanted to see them.

Chance rode the elevator to a suite on the third floor, praying for courage and strength. When he knocked on the door, he couldn't help but wonder if he would make matters worse.

Margaret Spencer opened the door. Her anxiety was evident in her eyes. "Mr. Randell."

"Mrs. Spencer. Thank you for seeing me," he said as he held his hat in his hands, grateful for something to hide his own nervousness. But all he needed to do was think about Joy and Katie and suddenly his strength was renewed.

James Spencer walked into the room, self-assured and arrogant. The man had to be hell in the boardroom. But this wasn't Spencer's territory. It was Randell's.

"Make it fast, Randell. I'm expecting a conference call."

Chance marched into the sitting area. He needed to stand face-to-face with this man, as if it were a shootout. "This isn't going to take long at all, Mr. Spencer. I just stopped by to let you know that if you try to take Katie away from Joy, you'll lose. Joy is a good mother, and she's made a home here in San Angelo. You may have connections in Denver, but you're in Texas now. We don't take kindly to strangers coming in and messing with our families. And Joy and Katie are my family."

Spencer looked taken aback, then quickly recovered. "That child is a Spencer," he insisted. "You can't take her away from me."

"The baby isn't yours to take," Chance argued. "She's Joy's daughter."

"And our son was her father."

Chance took aim and fired back. "A son you hadn't had anything to do with for years. Why would you want his child?"

Spencer looked flustered. "The relationship between me and my son is none of your business."

Another shot. "It will be the court's business if you proceed with this. I'm sure the judge would be interested to know that you and Blake hadn't been on speaking terms for years. And when he came to you for financial help when his wife was pregnant, you refused him.''

James Spencer paled.

''Yeah, Joy told me about your relationship with your son.''

''You…you can't threaten me.''

''You aren't giving me a choice. You threatened the two people I love.''

''Get the hell out of here.''

''Just be warned, Mr. Spencer, I'm going to spend every penny I have fighting you in court. You're not taking my family away.''

''You don't have anywhere near the assets I do. I could ruin you financially.''

For once in his life, Chance didn't care about losing everything he'd once valued. All he wanted was Joy and Katie. ''But I'll have something much more precious than money.''

He'd turned to walk away when Margaret Spencer came hurrying after him. ''Mr. Randell, please don't leave,'' she called.

The panic in her voice caused Chance to stop.

She glanced at her husband. ''Jim, please, I've gone along with you on a lot of things. I even lost my son because of your stubbornness. I can't lose my only grandchild. You will drop the suit.'' Her hands and voice were trembling. ''If not, you will lose so much more. Me and half your precious assets.''

A look was exchanged between the two, then Margaret turned back to Chance. ''Tell Joy I'm sorry for all the trouble we've caused her. I never wanted it to come to this. And if she can find it in her heart to forgive me, maybe she'll allow me just to see the baby...." Tears ran down her cheeks. "I would be so grateful."

Chance couldn't help but feel for the woman. "It's not my place to say, but I'll talk to Joy."

"Bless you, Mr. Randell. I'll be staying in town another few days. Please call."

Excitement raced through him as Chance walked out, his thoughts on getting home to Joy. But would she welcome him back? How could he expect her to open her arms to him when he'd walked out so many times?

He released a long breath. He'd just have to think of a way.

Joy walked the length of the kitchen and back. Katie was down for her nap, and there had been entirely too much time for her to think. In the last few hours Joy's whole life had seemed to fall apart. Chance was gone, and she could possibly lose her daughter.

Joy knew from talking to her lawyer that the Spencers' threats were bogus. But they could keep dragging her and Katie back to court for years. She'd be watched constantly, her parenting skills scrutinized. And worst of all, she and Katie would be alone.

How could this be happening? All she'd wanted was a home...a family. And for a few wonderful moments when she'd been in Chance's arms, he'd made her feel that it was all going to come true. But not any more.

Tears filled her eyes, and she tried to blink them away, but it was useless. Well, why not have a good cry? Her life was in shambles. And she was alone again.

Well, she couldn't stay here anymore, not with all

the memories. She'd have to sell the ranch. Wasn't that what Chance had wanted all along? Not her.

Joy looked around the old house that she'd lived in only six short weeks, but it sure felt like home to her. It didn't matter if the kitchen was archaic, the wallpaper faded, most of the steps on the staircase squeaked and the hardwood floors needed refinishing. She loved the place. But most of all she loved one stubborn cowboy. But he, like everyone else in her life, had left her....

At the sound of a truck pulling in the drive, Joy quickly wiped away her tears. It was probably Hank stopping by. He'd been out looking for Chance. When she looked up she discovered it wasn't Hank standing in the doorway, but Chance.

A warm flutter erupted in her stomach as she eyed the man in fitted jeans and a starched tan shirt that showed off his perfect shoulders. Shoulders that she'd rested her head on as he held her. Her gaze went to his clean-shaven jaw and his gray eyes, as piercing and as powerful as he was. He swept off his Stetson and held it in his hands as if waiting for her to speak first.

Well, fine. She'd get this over with. With the last of her pride, Joy squared her shoulders. "If you've come for your clothes, please be quiet. Katie is sleeping."

"I didn't come for my clothes," he said. "I came to talk, if you will let me."

"Why, so you can tell me more about why we don't work?" She shook her head. "No, Chance, spare me the explanations. We had a contract. You lived up to it. And I've decided to sell you the ranch. Katie and I will move into town."

He frowned. "But you love it here."

"I can't afford it anymore. James Spencer will have me in court, and I'll need money to fight him."

"No you won't. The Spencers aren't going to fight for custody."

Joy opened her mouth to speak, afraid she hadn't heard him right. "How? Why?"

"Let's just say that Margaret Spencer talked her husband out of the suit. She would like you to call her, hopes you'll let her see Katie. I told her that was up to you."

Joy was in shock. "What…what changed their minds?"

Chance shrugged. "I paid them a visit and set them straight on what a good mother you are…and told them that I'd fight them with everything I had."

Joy couldn't breathe, her heart was drumming in her chest. "You went to them? But I thought…."

Chance stopped her. He needed to have his say, let her know his feelings. "I was wrong, Joy. I admit I was scared that my past would hurt you and Katie, but I realized I don't have to take the blame for my daddy's sins. That I have a worth of my own. I've made a good name for myself. I could be a good father to Katie."

"I always knew that," she said. "From the beginning, you've been there for us." Joy swallowed. "You're the only father Katie has ever known. She…loves you."

"And I love her," he said, his voice a throaty whisper. God, to think he'd nearly walked away from it all.

Then Chance crossed to Joy. She raised her hand.

"Chance, please. I don't want to do this again. You've left me twice and could leave again."

Chance couldn't blame Joy for her mistrust. He'd given her plenty of reason. But he couldn't lose her. "I know I don't deserve another chance, but can you at least hear me out?"

Finally Joy nodded.

Chance released a breath as he drank in her beauty. Yellow hair curled around her pretty face. Her blue eyes mesmerized him. He had trouble thinking, let alone trying to tell her his true feelings. But he had to try. He reached for the contract in his back pocket and handed it to her.

"Here, I want you to have this back. And for you to tear it up. You were right, a contract marriage doesn't work." He saw the hurt on her face and he couldn't stand it. "I don't want this contract between us, Joy. I want a real marriage."

There was a flash of hope in her eyes, then she said, "You don't need to be married to me any longer, Chance. I said I would sell you the land. I know how much this place means to you."

"No, Joy, I don't want it. I do want you and Katie, though. I want us to be a family." He gripped her by the arms. She tried to pull away, but he wouldn't let her. "I love you."

She stopped her struggle. "You love me?"

He nodded slowly. "I've wanted to tell you for so long, but I was afraid. I know that you probably can't feel the same way about me as you did with your first husband, and I'd never try to take his place. But I'm as good a man as he. I can make us a good life here. I just want another chance to be your husband and Katie's father."

Joy raised her finger to his lips. "Stop right there, Chance Randell. First off, I don't want you to replace Blake. There will always be a place for him in my heart, but he's gone. I told you I closed that chapter of my life. I admit that at first I was scared. But I realized I was only frightened because what I felt for you was so overwhelming. Oh, Chance, I love you so much—"

Chance took her mouth with a kiss that nearly swept them away. He tried to show her how desperate he'd been for her. Over the past hours he'd realized she was the woman he was meant to love, and he craved her clear down to his soul.

He broke off the kiss, then leaned his forehead against hers. "Please, say you'll give me another chance."

Joy ran her fingertips along his arm, causing a shudder to run through him. "I don't know, cowboy. You'll have to talk to our daughter, and she's been pretty upset all day."

He smiled, loving the word *our*. "Oh, I think she'll forgive me. Wait until she sees the gift I brought her."

Joy laughed. "Trying to buy her affections?"

The wonderful sound was like music, and Chance skimmed his lips over her face, wrapping his hands under her hair at the nape of her neck. "Honey, I've missed you. I thought I'd never be able to hold you, make love to you ever again."

"Oh, Chance." She flung her arms around his neck and kissed him back.

Chance's body stirred, desperate with an ache that only Joy could satisfy. But he couldn't think about making love with her, not yet. He broke off the kiss. "We need to talk, Joy."

He whipped out another paper. "Here."

Joy didn't want to talk anymore. She wanted to make love to her husband. "What's this?" She opened the paper and began to read. It was another contract.

"I want us to be partners in everything," he said. "I want to buy into this ranch."

"But I already own it, and you're my husband."

He shook his head. "That's not how I do things. I can't live off you, Joy. Now, I've saved some money over the years, and I have a lot invested in horses. The income we get from horse breeding and training can make us a good living."

Joy went over the paper, impressed by the money he'd made. And the astronomical amount he got for stud fees.

"I want to do some remodeling in the house, and this kitchen is the first place we'll start. New flooring and appliances are a must. I'd also like to come up with a new name for the ranch. "How about the Triple R for the three of us?"

Joy's head was spinning. "But what about when we have more children?"

She bit back a smile when she saw the look on his face.

"You want children?" he asked.

Nodding, she went into his arms. "A few more. What about you?"

He cupped her face in his large hands. "Joy Randell, I love you. And I'd like nothing more then to carry you upstairs and make you pregnant this minute."

She wiggled her eyebrows. "A wonderful thought, cowboy, but could we postpone that idea a few months? I mean, Katie is still a baby. Maybe when she's a year old.''

He grinned. ''As long as we can practice.''

''Always.'' She was kissing him again when they heard the baby cry out.

''Sounds like someone is awake,'' Chance said. ''Why don't you go get her and bring her to the barn. That's where I have that surprise I promised.''

Joy fed Katie then changed her diaper in record time. With Ginger and Sunny following her, Joy carried her daughter to the barn, anxious herself to see the surprise. When Joy heard a horse whinnying her excitement grew. She called to her husband.

''Out here.''

Joy followed his voice to the opened double doors that led to the corral. She stopped with a gasp. Chance held the reins of the cutest butterscotch-colored pony. ''Oh, Chance, it's adorable.''

''Her name is Daisy. I bought her from the Campbells. Every one of their kids learned to ride on her. She's gentle as a lamb. Katie can learn on her until she's old enough for a real horse.''

There was no doubt about it, her husband was the sweetest man in the world. ''Don't you think she's a little young for a pony?''

Chance's silver gaze never wavered from hers. ''I want both the women in my life to know I'm sticking around. I'm through running, Joy. I'm never going to leave you again. I know how important it is to you to have a home. I want to make one here with you and Katie.''

He tied the pony's rein to the railing. ''Tomorrow, I'll bring over my horses from the Circle B. I have a sweet chestnut mare I picked out for you. They don't come any gentler than Glory Girl. I trained her myself. I'll teach you to ride like a true Texan.''

He took Katie from Joy. "Hello princess. Daddy's home.''

Katie cooed and waved her arms as Chance laid her against his shoulder. His hand rested against her back, and he whispered in her tiny ear. "I've missed you. But Daddy's here for good now.''

He pulled Joy to his side. "I don't think it can get any more perfect than this.''

"No, it can't,'' she agreed.

Joy knew that Chance had come a long way, trusting her, trusting her love. She had, too. Now they had each other and a place they could always call home. In each other's arms.

Epilogue

"Oh, this is beautiful," Joy breathed.

Chance glanced at his wife as she sat on horseback, her eyes filled with awe as she saw Mustang Valley for the first time.

The meadow's high grass was a rich green from the recent rains and huge oak trees lined the stream that ran along the edge of the Circle B property.

Smiling, Joy turned toward him. "When you said you wanted to take me riding, I had no idea.... This is where you and your brothers used to come, isn't it?"

"Yeah," he said. Chance took the lead down the gentle rise, but kept an eye over his shoulder as Joy followed with her chestnut mare. She sat relaxed in the saddle, reins held in her capable hand, expertly controlling her mount. He smiled to himself. Over the past two months she had worked hard, riding every day. She'd turned out to be a natural.

At the stream, Chance climbed down, and went to

help Joy. He lifted her from the saddle, but refused to release her.

"So, cowboy, did you bring me here to have your way with me?"

Grinning, he placed a kiss on her mouth. "The thought may have crossed my mind. How often have we been alone the past month? I hate to waste an afternoon when Ella's baby-sitting."

"Well, you better feed me first. I'm starving." Taking Glory's reins, she walked toward the stream.

Chance couldn't help but notice how different Joy was. She fit in to ranch life perfectly, dressed in her worn jeans and dusty boots. He needed to take her shopping again.

At the water's edge, Joy turned around and pulled off her hat and brushed the hair from her flushed face. "Thanks," she said. "For all the time you've taken to teach me to ride. I know it hasn't been easy, especially since I took you away from your horse training."

"You're important to me," he said as he let Ace drink. He untied the saddle blanket and a canvas bag filled with sandwiches and put them under a tree. "And you wanted to learn to ride, and you wanted it fast." Unable to resist her any longer, he pulled her into his arms. "Don't you know by now that slow and easy can be just as much fun?" He cocked an eyebrow. "How 'bout I give you another lesson?" he suggested.

Joy reached up and tangled her fingers in his hair, pushing off his hat as her lips met his in a searing kiss. One kiss led to another, lunch was forgotten, and they were on the blanket.

"I love you, Mrs. Randell," he said, taking another

kiss. Joy didn't resist as he leaned her back on the blanket.

"I love you, too, Mr. Randell, but as much as I'd like to show you, we can't. Ella is watching Katie."

"And she's loving every minute of it," Chance said. "This is our afternoon—alone." He bent his head and kissed her, leaving no doubt of his intentions.

"Oh, Chance," she whispered, trying to catch her breath. "You are making your point, but really, I promised Ella I'd help her finish up things for Hank's party this weekend."

"I hope Hank appreciates all the sacrifices," Chance said.

"I think he will." There was a twinkle in her eyes. "Especially if our out-of-town guests arrive. Hope you don't mind them staying at our house."

Chance loved the words *our house*. He thought back to when he and Joy had decided on the new name for their home—Randell Family Ranch.

"Oh, Chance, look," Joy whispered as she turned around, resting her head against his chest.

Chance followed her gaze and spotted a small herd of mustangs coming toward the stream about a half mile down. So they had come back. This time there were two new buckskin colts, hanging close to their mothers. He felt his emotions surfacing, but he didn't fight them anymore, not with Joy.

"When Cade, Travis and I were kids, we'd come here because it was a place where we thought we fit in. We identified with those ponies." He nodded. "Like us, they were misfits, a nuisance to ranchers. But Hank said they belonged here in this valley. And as long as he was around, the mustangs had a home." Chance's voice turned husky. "And so did we."

Joy's hand touched his jaw. "I promise you, Chance, I will love you so much you'll never feel that way ever again."

Chance stopped his wife's words with a kiss. "I'm a lucky man to have so much. You…Katie." He pulled Joy into his arms, unable to stop thinking about all he had. But what about Cade and Travis? Had they found love and happiness? "Joy. I wonder if my brothers are happy?"

"Don't they tell you about their lives?"

He shrugged. "Hank gets calls now and then. Travis stopped home about two years ago, but only stayed a day. He said he had to get back to his computer business. Cade hasn't been home since he left eight years ago. I understand. The girl he loved left him and married someone else. I went to Chicago once, but couldn't handle the big city and never went back."

"Feeling a little guilty?"

He smiled. "Yeah, I guess I am. I thought sending them off to college would give them a good start. Away from here and all the bad memories. Maybe I was wrong."

"Then contact your brothers and tell them how much you want them home. You might be surprised what happens."

Chance looked at her curiously. She was up to something. Just then a rider appeared on the rise. Chance sat up and focused on the stranger riding Circle B stock. The closer he came the more familiar he seemed. Then Chance's heart began to pound. The rider made his way to them and climbed off his horse. He stood over six feet and his hair was darker than Chance's own. When the man walked toward them, his slow lazy gait caused Chance to suck in a breath. Cade? He turned to Joy.

"Why don't you go and say hello to Cade?"

Chance didn't hesitate. He ran over and pulled his brother into a rough embrace. "Cade. Damn, it's good to see you."

"Good to see you, too, bro."

"What the hell you doing here?"

"I came back for Hank's party. Ella wanted to surprise him." Cade stood back and smiled, but there was a loneliness Chance recognized in the other man's eyes. His brother wasn't as happy as he pretended. "I hear you got yourself married."

Just then Joy came up to them. "Hi Cade, it's good to finally meet you." She hugged him.

"It's good to meet you." He glanced at his brother. "You'll have to tell me how you got such a pretty gal."

"I've got two," Chance said, unable to stop grinning. "There's a little one back at the house."

"I already got a peek at Katie. She's real pretty." He smiled. "They must be special ladies to hog-tie you." He glanced around. "And you brought her out here to sacred ground."

Chance knew Cade was teasing him about the promise they'd made. "Since my brothers weren't around, I didn't think anyone would mind. Hey, is Travis going to make the party?"

Both men looked at Joy.

"He said he'd try his best," she said.

Chance hugged his wife. "Well, let's go back to the house and call him."

Cade mounted up as Joy and Chance gathered their things.

"Thank you," Chance said. "But how did you get him to come?" he asked.

"How do you think?" She grinned. "I sweet-talked him."

Chance grabbed his wife. "From now on, Mrs Randell, I'm the only one you sweet-talk."

She laced her fingers around his neck, raised up and kissed him. Her lips were soft, yet demanding, making him forget everything except her. "It would be my pleasure." Joy glanced at the man at the top of the rise. "Later," she promised.

Chance had no doubt that this woman would keep her word. She had made a guy like him believe that he could have it all. All the love and family he could stand.

* * * * *

Look for more of

THE TEXAS BROTHERHOOD

in Silhouette Romance with Patricia Thayer's

A CHILD FOR CADE

June 2001

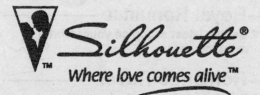

Don't miss the reprisal of
Silhouette Romance's popular miniseries

When King Michael of Edenbourg goes missing, his devoted family and loyal subjects make it their mission to bring him home safely!

Their search begins March 2001 and continues through June 2001.

On sale March 2001: **THE EXPECTANT PRINCESS**
by bestselling author **Stella Bagwell** (SR #1504)

On sale April 2001: **THE BLACKSHEEP PRINCE'S BRIDE**
by rising star **Martha Shields** (SR #1510)

On sale May 2001: **CODE NAME: PRINCE**
by popular author **Valerie Parv** (SR #1516)

On sale June 2001: **AN OFFICER AND A PRINCESS**
by award-winning author **Carla Cassidy** (SR #1522)

Available at your favorite retail outlet.

Where love comes alive™

SILHOUETTE *Romance*

COMING NEXT MONTH

#1522 AN OFFICER AND A PRINCESS—Carla Cassidy
Royally Wed: The Stanburys
Military law forbade their relationship, but couldn't stop the feelings
Adam Sinclair and Princess Isabel Stanbury secretly harbored. Could
they rescue the king, uncover the conspirators—*and* find the happily-
ever-after they yearned for?

#1523 HER TYCOON BOSS—Karen Rose Smith
25th Book
Mac Nightwalker was wary of gold-digging women, but struggling
single mom Dina Corcoran's money woes touched the cynical tycoon.
He offered her a housekeeping job, and Dina quickly turned Mac's
house into the home he'd never had. Did the brooding bachelor dare let
his Cinderella slip away?

#1524 A CHILD FOR CADE—Patricia Thayer
The Texas Brotherhood
Years earlier, Abby Garson had followed her father's wishes and
married another, although her heart belonged to Cade Randell. Now
Cade was back in Texas. But Abby had been keeping a *big* secret
about the little boy Cade was becoming very attached to....

#1525 THE BABY SEASON—Alice Sharpe
An Older Man
Babies, babies everywhere! A population explosion at Jack Wheeler's
ranch didn't thrill producer Roxanne Salyer—she didn't think she was
mommy material. But Jack's little girl didn't find anything lacking in
Roxanne's charms, and neither did the divorced doctor daddy....

#1526 BLIND-DATE BRIDE—Myrna Mackenzie
Tired of fielding the prospective husbands her matchmaking brothers
tossed her way, Lilah Austin asked Tyler Westlake to be her pretend
beau. Then Tyler realized that he didn't want anyone to claim Lilah
but him! What was a determined bachelor to do...?

#1527 THE LITTLEST WRANGLER—Belinda Barnes
They'd shared a night of passion—and a son James Scott knew
nothing about. Until Kelly Matthews showed up with a toddler—
the spitting image of his daddy! When the time came for Kelly to
return to college, could James convince her he wanted both of them
to stay...forever?

RSCNM0501